D1825780

THREE KING MACKEREL AND A MAHI MAHI

carolineclemens.com

Also By Caroline Clemens

Into the Vines
Brie's Story
Someday
The Pilot Log
Autumn Quotes
String the Cranberries
Chocolate for Lilly

Caroline Clemens

THREE KING MACKEREL AND A MAHI MAHI

THREE KING MACKEREL AND A MAHI MAHI

For information about special discounts available for bulk
purchases, sales promotions, fund- raising and educational
needs, contact:

Clemensnovels
https://carolineclemens.com/

ISBN 978-1-37007366-5
ISBN 978-1-64316-652-0

Cover Design by Daniela Owergoor from Brazil
This novel is a work of fiction. Names, places, businesses,
events, buildings, people, and circumstances are either
used fictitiously, or are the author's imagination to build
creatively.

This book is dedicated to my grandfather, *Gilbert Clemens*, who was known as the ultimate storyteller and poet. He's likely the first male in my life that allowed me, possibly, to get away with my desires (like combing & styling his hair relentlessly). Writing has become one of my desires.

THREE KING MACKEREL AND A MAHI MAHI

PROLOGUE

What do you do with a $52 billion dollar budget? You hire contractors to fill in slots wherever you need them-even overseas.

Then one day a contractor born on June 21st 1983 with an IQ greater than 145 sees something amiss then tells three separate people. After all, he comes from a good family, servicemen from the Coast Guard, and even has a sister who's a lawyer.

But to his chagrin no one listens, he decides to flee and contacts a reporter to inform what he believes is wrong doing. Snowden is on the run in an airport without a country reveals the national headlines. This surveillance the country learns is called PRISM, going in the back door of six major companies and doesn't seem fair to the American people. Do they even know about it? Will anyone care about Edward Snowden after June 10, 2013? And why should we? If you aren't disobeying the law as a citizen then why should you care what the government is doing to keep you safe? Seems legit; seems fair.

He made a decision and became a whistleblower, forever altering his life and those unsuspecting women back in 2013. Who are those women no one knows about? This novel of fiction explores an idea.

CHAPTER ONE

When I check my watch I have five minutes left to be on time; my phone says I'm sixminutes away. I glance in the rear view mirror and smile at myself. I'm never late. First impressions are gone now for my appointment. I increase the volume to my Sirius station fifty-one bpm and listen to a new remix. I'll be on time, I repeat to myself, as I give the pedal a push.

"Turn right in ninety feet onto Silo Street," says the lady from maps.

I pull in following the instructions and find a nearby parking spot out front then quickly shut off the engne. The place seems rather empty save for three cars. Someone passes by on the sidewalk, and I nod quickly noticing there's nothing out back but fields and a few old tin roofed worn houses. Green's Tavern was an out of the way bar in a small isolated, unused town in North Georgia. I quickly apply a small dose of fuchsia lipstick. Lips match my shirt, you go girl.

Quiet heart, don't get excited, you've not even met the guy yet. Nice going Megan, I think to myself.

Here goes nothing as I shake off any doubts. I open the door to the tavern and take a quick deep breathe to saturate my lung cells, areoles-something I remember from my medical terminology class I took in my first year of college, then exhale.

Actually, I can't wait to meet him. I'm hoping he matches his great profile. How could anyone be so good looking?

First blind date I think, *yup, right off the internet dating service Single in ATL.*

I could see him over to the left at a small table as soon as I walk through the door. I press the button on my phone for the time. My cell says 2:00. Perfect. He stands up to acknowledge me as I enter the place. Sweet Jesus, he has manners. I smile.

"Megan?" James questions.

"James?" I answer with a question.

"Yes. You found this little hideaway?" This gorgeous man in front of me asks.

"Maps. Quaint inside though, like something from the old days." I ramble on mesmerized for a moment.

"Yes. That's exactly how I would describe it. Come on over here, there's a bit of privacy, albeit with a mirror back drop."

At first we sit across from each other, exchange a few niceties, and order a couple beers. There's a long bar at one side which is across from us, then there are small booths and tables scattered about in a rustic setting in the middle of the place. I could imagine a western being filmed inside this place.

We discuss the making of our profiles for the dating site and the questions we previously answered. We both said we liked the site because they left the asking of questions up to us. In fact, instead of knowing too much they preferred simple basics. So here we were. I ask him why he chose a dating service.

"I'm older, bars are great for sure. When you are young

and waiting for that special person to walk over to you, or vice versa, it makes sense. Now I'd like to have conversation along with my drink and not wait until the end of the evening, even if it's someone I never want to see again. Make sense?"

"Oh, I get that completely." I reply. Even though it's been forever since I dated, I did briefly before getting married.

"Why did you sign on?" James questions me.

"My time is very limited as I have obligations with work and family." I told him this without blurting out the kid factor. A friend told me once you can tell them just not at first. They are there to date you, to see if they like you first. The family comes soon but not at first. I took this advice.

The front door opens and two guys walk in headed for the long bar. I see that James takes note of this. That's the funny thing about blind dates, you find yourself watching every little nuance.

Relax Megan, *it's just a date. Don't think about your to-do list for two hours. Got it? Right.*

James asks to sit next to me. This took me by surprise. He watches the two men take stools at the bar, there's only one other person sitting at the end of the bar near the exit out back. The juke box is playing country tunes as they twang at my heart. I reply with uncertainty, "Yes."

I scoot in towards the mirror then turn to face my date, my blind date I've just met. The waiter from the back comes and takes our order of burger, fries, grilled cheese, and fried green tomatoes after he sets down our two beers.

James turns towards me to focus on me, I suppose, and I laugh a little then stare back at him for a moment too. We talk about our jobs and I tell him about being a lifeguard last summer at a local neighborhood pool.

"A lifeguard?" He asks.

"Well, it was right after my divorce, and I hadn't worked in a while. I felt kind of lost, and still had these skills from my competition swim days."

"Impressive. How did the job go?"

"Like going back in time without all the fuss. Just imagine if you took a job at an ice cream parlor, only you weren't seventeen anymore trying to impress your friends and make contacts. You were now twenty seven, knowledgeable, confident, been there-done that, don't care what anyone thinks of you attitude." I laughed.

"I get it. You know guys graduate emotionally too. They like their buddies for a long time, even though they want the girl real bad. Once they get over the, I got one, do you have one yet? Everything gets better."

"When did that happen for you?"

"I suppose after my nineteenth birthday I lessened my need to have her no matter what."

I concentrate on my food for a moment and find myself enjoying this blind date. He does match his profile, and his voice is deep, with concern and a light laugh that mellows him. Deep brown eyes and light brown straight hair frame his face with lips I might want to kiss. I was beginning to feel an attraction in this short time. I let it go.

We eat half our lunch and begin sharing more information.

Sitting rather close we talk about personal issues like 'do I have kids?' That's one of those questions the service leaves blank as they've determined it can be a turn off for couples that really might be compatible. What's compatible anyway I think? Don't opposites attract?

"I have three boys." Finally, I blurt it out.

"Really? How old are they? What are their names?"

I'm immediately calmed by his questions and we continue this great conversation.

Suddenly, James, comes really close and pulls me to him as he kisses me. Whoa. I close my eyes and am not sure what's happening. This seems a little forced. I wait. And wait. And wait some more. Then when he stops I open my eyes and see that James is focused on the mirror behind me.

I pull back slightly. "Tell me what you're looking at?"

"Not at myself, dear. There's an exchange going on behind me." He whispers directly at me with piercing eyes and a seriousness reserved for when you got in trouble as a kid.

I look at him and scope his face over for a clue. "What are you, a cop?"

"You mean like undercover?"

"Yes, that kind?"

"No."

I pull away and eat another bite realizing I'll need another beer. I flag the bartender for another and he brings it over. James pays the bill, tip included. He watches one of the guys exit towards the back. The bartender points and signals to go left and further out. James kisses me again-with both hands and messes up my hair. I hear the country music with that familiar twanging voice banging hard. He parts from my lips and whispers in my ear, "Feel like being an outlaw just a wee bit?"

"No."

"You need to do as I say so we can get out of here. There's a bad exchange going down and it's not going to be pretty. I need you to do as I say, okay?"

CHAPTER TWO

I stare out the front window and wonder what the bartender put in my beer? I've been kissed. Now I'm told to obey someone I just met. I shake my head and think of my three boys. I'm coming home to y'all but, somehow, I do believe this stranger has a hold on me. The stranger that I just met on my blind date. James Edward Kelly is 33 years of age from Tampa, Florida, never married, 6'2" with thick brown hair, brown eyes, tan skin, and a scar near his right carotid artery from a dog bite. He is of Mexican-Irish descent, way back. I rehearse the details info from the dating site. But today in person with a red plaid shirt on-he's plain gorgeous.

"You forgot to click the outlaw button on the dating site," I whisper.

"Let's go. You see the other guy is leaving out the front?"

"Yes." I say not sure if I want to be a part of this plan he is forming.

"As soon as he gets out the front door, we go where the coat is, you reach in and get the envelope. I'll cover you, then we walk like lovers out the front door and make haste."

"That's it? Then what?" Am I really going to participate in this obvious bad guys business?

"We hope we don't get chased." James states matter-of-factly. This makes me tense but I have no time to think. We must react. "By the way the description you left on the site is way underdone."

"He's cleared the front door." I state and wonder what he means by that last statement.

"Up we go." James is in control. I can tell this is not his first time following a sting or whatever undercover malarkey this is.

Maybe, I was in a movie, I thought. I followed James and walked to the bar top as James was all over me cuddling, touching, and acting like he couldn't keep his hands off me. I smile at the bartender, like yeah, I'm in love. Then I pretend to reach down and scratch my knee, putting my hand in the pocket of the coat which is draped over the now empty chair. What if the dude comes back from the jon? I mean the outhouse out back? I grab a thick envelope, no time to look at its contents. I put this in my purse with one fell swoop, then kiss my would-be lover, and put my shades on. Arm and arm, we hurry out the front door.

That's when we hear the loud explosion. It shook us and we momentarily hold each other more tightly. The sound came from behind the bar towards the fields with the old worn houses covered in kudzu. We couldn't see anything yet. Nothing had to tell us to run. We just did, towards James car.

James wanted to slam the door shut. I could tell, but he closes it after I jump in and stare out the front window. I feel trapped in time as it takes only seconds for us to escape. What are we escaping from? My heart beats and jumps close to my skin while my brain is fluid. It knows the next step is to listen for instructions. My date apparently knows what he's doing. Damn. Maybe I should have tried another agency with more questions. No time to wish for what wasn't occurring. Remain in the here and now, Megan.

Excitement … I pause to consider this. Haven't you been wanting a life outside of the kids?

Hurrying with sprint like steps he runs to the driver's side, slides in, and starts the engine. He glances behind us then pulls out with the gas pedal to the floor. I hit the right side, and then wholly toss over to the left. *Get a grip* I tell myself. He's driving fast and there is no stopping.

Once on the main road-I see him check the rear view mirror more than once. Was he looking for the guy who walked out the front? Something told me this was serious. So serious that I should keep my mouth shut until we get to where he wants to go. I gave it three seconds to wonder where that might be. Then I sigh and take a deep breath.

He did seem to be a good driver.

"My car," I say.

"I know. I'm going to send someone for it."

"You're a movie star and you cannot tell anyone!" I exclaim.

"Nice try," James laughs and then continues, "Megan with the lovely green eyes and gorgeous long dark blonde hair which frames a strong face who is built like a goddess! She's from Huron, Ohio and steps out at 125 lbs. sporting toned legs with a 5'8" athletic physique."

"You forgot 27 years of age with the Scandinavian descent!" We both want to laugh at ourselves but can't. "I'm scared."

"Megan with the three boys, I'm returning you to them. Trust me."

Okay. Yup, this is serious. I wonder if I should be worried, like for my life or something. I told myself *if I should be worried about my life, then I would be.* If I had to question my own self, then bullshit. Don't be. Later when we get to safety I'm giving him my best lecture shit I got!

We turn right, drive awhile, and then turn left. Fields of grass, rolling hills with an occasional kudzu explosion near an intersection was all there was out here. That and very old houses, barely standing and certainly swaying to one side.

We stop. He then takes off with an extra explosion of power but he has to curve to the left over the line as we nearly miss a guy mowing his lawn. Time seems to slow down like the last 30 seconds of your life, all in a second and a half. From the side of the road, eyes that stare and bulge from his sockets, relate his expressed vision of distaste directly at us. We nearly hit him, just missing his tortured bony body with long, wild curly hair by a grass blade.

"What the hell was that?" I ask for both of us.

"Oh man, he's scary. I've seen him before; he likes to scare the cars by leaning over into the street like he wants to get hit or something," James replies.

"I think he's on crack or whatever is the latest chemical sold on the street. Crazy!"

"I'm sorry. You okay? Seriously, not everyone is debilitated out here in the country. Look who you're with." He lifts his eyebrows up and down, and follows this with a wink and light laugh.

I had to stare. Then I laugh out loud. Once I was composed I had to ask, "Who am I with?"

"You're about to find out. I'll show you very soon. I promise." My Mysterious Man Date Named James is the title of the movie I'm in. At least the dating service has his driver's license so my kids will know who killed me. Boy this will be a big story in the Journal-except I want life with my kids for a while yet. I want to laugh but my body just shivers and goosebumps pop out on my arms and legs. Your body doesn't lie. I'm in the fight or flight syndrome and about to throw myself out of this car!

I see him calm down after we are about seven miles or so away from the Tavern. I blink my eyes, lick my lips, and decidedly speak, "You going to fill me in or should I guess what just happened back on our lunch date?" I straighten out my neck and turn my head from shoulder to shoulder to loosen up the tension that heightened our first kiss.

James turns and smiles at me. Oh such a cute smile, that I reply in like.

I stare at him, he looks back into the mirror, then pauses with a long look at me. "I most certainly have much to tell you. Do you like BBQ?"

"Sure but I just ate." My sarcasm is dead on, kind of like the dude back at the bar.

Did I just witness a murder? I wonder.

"We'll hang out in there." He points to a small log type building. "Order, then take it to go. Sound good?"

"My car." I remind him.

"I will have it delivered to my place. Okay?"

"You live nearby?"

"Fairly close."

He pulls into a gravel drive followed by a parking lot, then drives around back completely out of site. I shake my head thinking there cannot be another shenanigan. No way.

"This is My Brother's Place," James whispers.

"Your brother's place?" I ask.

"No, not my brother's place but somebody else's Brother's Place."

"That's what I said didn't I?"

We burst out laughing.

"That's not what you said."

"I know."

James laughs some more. "Hey, I'm sorry for the beginning of this date but please come in and we'll talk at

'My Brother's Place' which happens to be my cousins BBQ place."

"Love to, I think." I look out the window. If nothing else this date is memorable, one for the notebook to read when I'm older. I think about my grandmother who wrote a book about her life. Some called it boring but I thought it fascinating to look back into the life of someone from a long time ago.

CHAPTER THREE

He hurries around the car again with a quick step, comes to my side and opens the door. He's such a gentleman. I step out and look at this good looking man with a smirk on his face. I'm thinking there's more. I just know it. This night, I mean day is not done. No way. He takes my hand.

We walk around to the front and go in through the screen door. I wonder if May is James's favorite month like me. The slight smack of the screen door hitting its frame alerts me to my favorite time of year besides Christmas. Smells delicious, even though I'm not hungry. It would make for a good supper.

"Take a look at the menu and we'll order it to-go if you like. You okay with that?"

"Sure." At this point I'm just trying to enjoy the ride and make it back home safe and sound. I don't ever have to go out with him again. I'm a big girl with kids and responsibilities. And summer is coming, even though I secretly wanted to have a summer boyfriend, I decide right here I can do without the hassle.

The place is cedar wood planks inside with a pine log home look on the outside. Very small and is quite quaint. James orders pulled pork with two sides to go then we help ourselves to a beer in the fridge sitting in the corner. James points to a small staircase in the corner, winding up to the second floor, more like a fire escape. I follow him as we ascend to the second level. No one is up here. *Cool place* I think to myself.

There's a jukebox in the corner and James pulls quarters out from his pocket and asks me if I have a preference, "Kenney Chesney, Old Blue Chair or Key Lime Pie?"

"Key Lime Pie," I say. Not sure why. Anything blue just didn't sound good since my divorce.

I find myself looking around at the pictures on the walls. The place is tiny up top here, three or four tables, jukebox, and a small dance floor. I knew what was coming next or did I?"

"Checkers?"

"Sure, you're going to lose though. I'm the Queen of game boards, all of them."

"Confident. Nice. Saddle up Miss Megan, I'm the King of I can do better when I want to!"

We settle into a few games of checkers. I won all of them and then we sit back and talk about us.

Actually, first up he tells me my car is already en route to his place. I nod in agreement. Am I on a date with James Bond I ponder?

"I thought you might worry about that."

"Tell me what's going on," I plead.

"I was a police officer for two years right out of high school. I saw deals go down and today looked like a deal going sour. I don't know I just had that feeling."

"You saw things like that in your past, like what New York City or something?" I had to ask the unbelievable. I continue on. "There was an explosion and I'm assuming that someone is probably dead, like the receiver of this!" I pull out the money envelope and open it. I begin to count.

"We don't know if he's dead, but probably. We didn't do anything bad Megan."

"No, we didn't. But who's the bad guy and who's the good guy? I can't see the difference. One guy gives another money, and I'm assuming for a job well done. Then the guy who gave the money likely explodes him to bits out back, leaves, and then comes back for the money! So who's bad? Both are maybe." I shake my head.

"That's a first impression. Think about it some more. Think bad ideas."

"This is not a paycheck. What do we do with this? And who gave it to him?"

"Now, you are asking the right questions, my dear."

I finished counting and exclaimed, "Nineteen thousand, eight hundred and forty, are you kidding me?"

"A bit Orwellian, I'd say. Or someone took a hundred and sixty dollar tip."

"You are not even shocked at this. Why?"

"I told you that old get into cop mode gear steps right in line. They taught us well."

"Okay, well, I'm a law abiding citizen so you take the envelope and handle whatever it is you think just happened. I have a family and don't need any of these outlaw … ish deeds happening to me. Got it?"

"Got it!"

"Good." I handed him the envelope with the money. Good. I was done. I was over it.

"Sex Pistols," I said.

"What?"

"I'd like to listen to Sex Pistols." I have no idea why I blurted that out but I did. I think I was slightly afraid at the moment. Shake it off Megan. Be strong. Be good.

"I'll check." James got up and went to search for an old

band my mother used to listen to when she was frightened. Rubbed off I guess.

What began playing was 'All About That Bass' by Meghan Trainor. I couldn't be more pleased.

"Dance with me," he says.

This was the little fun that I needed. We twirl around acting more like we are at a square dance in high school gym class than anything else. We dance in the moment and no one can take that away from me.

The owner pops his head up the stairs and brings us some popcorn. We sit and listen to more tunes and talk about our past, slighted relationships, and then my kids. I went on and on.

"Ian, he's eight. Matthew and Patrick are twins and are almost seven. They'll be seven in July, in about six weeks."

"You are a busy lady, I'm sure. No wonder the online dating service. Are they into sports?"

"For sure, little league baseball in the fall, soccer in the spring, and church basketball complete Saturday mornings during the winter. We go and go, all the time. Sundays, though, I stop the clock and its total downtime. I make everyone stay home, read, do homework, watch TV, and help me to make a big Sunday dinner!"

"I would like to come to that."

"Sometimes we watch a movie in our jammies," I add.

"I'd like that, too." James stands up and takes my hand. "Let's dance again."

The music is slower and I can hear Kenney Chesney's song 'Key Lime Pie' getting going. We dance to this light country-ocean ballad and I feel calm moving around the small dance floor. Once again I am mesmerized and don't question my closeness to this man in front of me. At the end I kiss him, and it's nice, slow and sweet, like the song.

After the dance we pause and James goes to check on the food downstairs, I gather myself and visit the little window in the middle of the room. I look out at the empty parking lot, after all it is the middle of the afternoon. Such excitement, fear, and wonder all in the spans of a couple hours. I don't think he's an outlaw post cop career. So what is he? I guess if I stick around I'll find out. For now I'm feeling rather cozy up top here at this little BBQ joint in the middle of north Georgia.

I take one more moment to look out at the stone covered empty parking lot and feel removed from reality. Could a person fall in love in a couple hours? In the movies they fall in love in two or three minutes, so I reckon anything is possible in this unreal afternoon.

After dancing some more we look at each other and finish the conversation on the busted deal at the tavern. "Give me your best guess about what happened Megan."

"From my perspective or a detective TV show?" I ask.

"First tell me how you saw it, then add the television flavor." James instructs.

"Two guys walk into a bar, one is a crook and the other is good. One is paying off the other for a job he did. One gives the other an envelope of money which the accepter stashes in his pocket. He forgets about it, being all happy, and goes to the jon. The payer exits the bar. Why? We don't know. Then there's an explosion and we see the guy who left the bar return to the bar. Did he plan to kill the guy he paid? Or is he as surprised as we are?"

"Now you are doing good, keeping an open mind. Except for one flaw," James critiques my take on the situation.

"What flaw?" I have to ask but actually am not sure I want to know.

"How do you know one is a crook and the other is

good?"

"Point made. Yes, I understand. We don't know if it was two good guys or two bad guys."

"Correct. And another flaw ..."

"Seriously, another?"

"We don't know if the job has been accomplished or it's for the future," James says.

"James, and another thought, we must remember the guy left the bar with his stash unattended. He trusted the guy who gave it to him."

"What does that tell you Megan?"

"It tells me the guy who gave the money is a double agent, trusted by the recipient. Poor dude who went to the outside jon."

"Don't even say poor dude."

"Why?"

"We don't even know if he is dead," James added. We both reflect.

"Maybe we're the bad dudes who took the money," I concede.

"Okay, don't go that far. We're good, at least I am," James laughs.

I laugh too. What else could I do at this point? I quietly reflect back to when my dad would ask my mom questions at home, while he tried to figure out a difficult case. He never knew I had listened in a few times. He would have been furious.

We get up to leave, exit down the spiral stairs, say goodbye to his cousin and find our car. The date ends well. I feel much better and wait for James to explain further.

James reassures me as we drive away to his place that he will take control of what has happened. He apologizes but tells me not to worry, that he used me as a cover when he kissed me quickly for whatever went down. He tells me to trust him. Should I? When I think about it I'm feeling overwhelmed by the situation and know that it's out of my league. I wouldn't know where to begin: except that we stole money from a pocket, we think the guy is dead, and we didn't kill him. Who did?

"You will read about it in the newspaper tomorrow, but it won't be the whole story. Don't tell anyone, only talk to me. Got that?"

"Yes, but you'll need to show me your papers if we are acting like important investigators on a television show." I wink at him and he acknowledges my words.

CHAPTER FOUR

We arrive at his place and walk inside. He heads into the kitchen and I follow him. He sets down the food from the BBQ place.

He pulls out a badge right before me. There it was. He was an undercover cop. I studied it.

"I don't date cops."

"Why not?" James asks.

"It's dangerous. I don't like danger. But I do like their protection, like today. I like that."

"I know someone has to do it, just don't let it be me." He returns.

"I have a confession."

"Yes. Tell me, if you want."

"My mom was married to a cop ... my dad. I loved him. He died."

Silence.

"We have something in common," he uttered quietly.

"What?"

"Mine died when I was nine, just old enough to know ... and love him."

Silence.

We sat there like lone wolves afraid of the dark, not knowing what to say, taking it all in. Taking in the impact of lives destroyed instantly by way of the badge. Reckless individuals who stopped the heartbeat of the protector, the one who would make a difference in helping, the lover of life, the fearless, or so many thought. How brave can one man be?

James went to warm up the take out dinner. I phone home to check on my kids. Everything was fine, the sitter said. I told her I'd be home in an hour. That was perfectly fine. She told me to have a great time and that two more hours would be okay. Fine.

We eat then watch a comedy special on TV. This seems fitting to ignore the earlier catastrophe and our part in escaping. Somehow, I wasn't too shaken, and that would be because James reassures me and holds me as we sit on his couch. I believe him. I saw his badge, his badge of courage.

Much later on I leave and he walks me outside to my car which had mysteriously showed up earlier via a tow truck. We linger on the driveway recapping our lunch date minus the episode, and on to the BBQ joint which was not his brother's place, rather My Brother's Place, and what were we doing later as in next week?

"Text me if you want to do something at the end of next week. Kids are in school for two more weeks then the load will lighten up until summer sets in."

"Definitely sounds great. I'd like to see you again Miss Megan."

"And I would like to see you." I decide to trust him. I've seen the badge, the badge of courage, and want to know more. I also decide he fits his profile; he's real in real life. Smiles.

I land in my car seat, breathe noticeably, and pull out my Tuscany mix. I need Bocelli to sing. I feel so alive! James leans down and kisses me again. He places his hand on my cheek tenderly and whispers a few words and asks if I'm okay? I reply yes by shaking my head, smile, and turn the engine on.

I take the long way home via the highway as I listen to words I don't even understand but feel in my heart. The night is real and so am I. My time off from being a mommy is as good as the time I am one. Life has blessed me I know this. Where I was going I didn't know? I didn't know my future but listening to a tenor sing about love made me know I wanted that.

CHAPTER FIVE

'*Explosion Out Back of Green's Tavern Shakes Small Community*' read the headline as I pick up the newspaper outside my door. I shake my head. What on earth have I gotten myself into?

The boys are eating breakfast at the counter. I lay the newspaper down away from them and reach into the fridge for some orange juice. As soon as I close the door Patrick asks, "How was your date momma?"

I look into his sweet brown eyes and think I'd love to tell him the scary story because he loves to be scared but I better not connect the dots for now. "I had a nice time, good BBQ, and even danced a little."

"You danced? Cool."

"Yeah, it was cool."

"Ian gets to go to a dance next week at school," said Matt. "He's going to dance with girls."

"Maybe," replied Ian.

"Maybe you'll go or maybe you'll dance with girls?" I ask.

"Both."

"I'd dance with the girls, especially that Lyndsay girl who likes you!" shouts Patrick.

"I guess that's your loss." Ian stood and cleared his

breakfast dishes. "Time for the bus. Let's go."

"I'll drive you guys today if you want," I say.

"Mom, I'd like that. Then I can finish my math problem before class."

I knew this was a distraction from reading the headlines. It's a good thing I didn't tell anyone where my lunch date was or I'd have a hundred questions. I like the chaotic calmness of the morning commute which I usually indulge in about two to three times a week. I find out quite a lot when nobody thinks I'm listening, or maybe the morning had an uncomplicated energy for communication. I don't know. I just love this time with my boys. I went straight home to read the paper after dropping them in the car line, saying good bye, and waving them off.

I pour myself a second cup of coffee and sit on the sofa with my feet up to read the paper. I didn't pause until I was through. The phone rang and I rose to answer it wondering if it would be James. It was.

"Hello Megan. Morning."

"Morning James."

"No nightmares?"

"None."

"Just checking. You read the paper or watched the news?"

"Yes, I read it. Not much there, no connections."

"You're smart. Except there is one connection."

"What's that?"

"Us."

"Oh yeah, I'm trying to forget."

"Sorry to remind you. Bad of me I guess."

"I suppose it will be one of those unsolved mysteries."

"Until I figure it out."

Silence. *Maybe I shouldn't carry on with this person* I thought.

"I know you don't date cops. Give me another chance. Okay?"

"I'll think about it. Okay."

"How about a movie? Or the county fair?"

"Movie first, then maybe the fair if all goes well."

"Movie. Saturday night say 6:30?"

"Perfect."

I take a shower and think about my future. Why don't I know what to do? Megan, likely it is because your marriage fell apart, and now you have three kids all under eight. You are a busy lady. Yes, but I want to capture a piece of the world for me, too. I had to admit, yesterday was exciting, but dangerous. What if the guy had come after James and I? What if he had followed us? Maybe he had. What if I was being tailed already? Well, I did nothing wrong. Oh wait a minute! I stole a bunch of money and gave it to James. He's in the wrong taking that money. Who does it belong to?

Suddenly, I know what I want to do. I want to solve mysteries. I want to use my brain and get the bad guys. If one watches the news and/or reads the papers, bad guys were everywhere. But I do not like danger. How can I get involved and not put myself in harm? I had a family to protect, watch over, and make sure we had a future. There must be a place for me. But guns? Yikes. I wasn't sure about guns or shooting them. My mind went to my dad who died in the line of the blue duty. He served his country and his community but life was cut short. *Maybe*, I thought, *I could help James by being a partner and serve my community behind the scenes*. Maybe there was a place for me. Maybe my future was happening right now. Maybe I was supposed to meet James. Okay-cut the crap, get moving Megan. Time to learn some bad ass ways. Get tough. But hey, my mom always said I had bad ass ways. What did she mean?

Saturday

I decide to give this date all I had. Tomorrow I would decide, yes or no, if I'd continue. My kids were at sleepovers by 4:30 and I had two hours to get in top shape. I shower, light a candle, pour a glass of wine and go to my closet to find some sexy, not mommy, outfit! What was that anyway?

Something sexy with a hot look as the boys like to say lately. Of course, they got everything off of the internet, TV, or friends. I had yet to get them a phone or iPad lap top etc. They played games at their friends' houses but I put that off until age ten for this house. *Woo hoo* I thought. *Great mom.* Ha ha. I sip my wine.

The doorbell rang. I grab my robe, swirl it on, and race to see who was there. I figure it would be someone wanting to play with the boys. My roommate and her child were away for a week or so. No one was there when I answer the door. Funny. Probably some kids doing a late afternoon-early evening dare, ring and run, as fast as you can.

As I look over a couple items to wear, holding them up in front of me to see in the mirror, it crosses my mind that my friend had told me to check my date out online. She said, "you know Megan, make sure he's legit, and not a serial killer or something." Well, she had a point but I didn't bother. I thought the agency likely did background checks but now I couldn't remember. Did they?

I choose the red dress, or as some would say the slut look. Seriously, in the old days like my mother's era, referring to a slut was a bad thing. Nowadays one wanted to portray the slut look. What's up? I think. Confusing. If I was going to catch this guy I might as well do it right away. First up, no holds bar, to see if we are made for each other. I laugh at myself. Red was just my color anyway with my dyed blonde hair and tan skin. I select my Brazilian leather strapped three inch summer shoes and gold round hoop earrings. Stunning I would say when I finished giving my hair a swirl. Makeup and sprays of perfume added in a couple places. I must admit this dating thing was quite fun. It certainly took my mind off all the kids, their activities, and my responsibility for them.

Six o'clock came and I was ready. I pour another half glass of wine and turn on the music. Maybe he would be early; should I text him I'm ready? I would.

This date tonight felt comfortable and right; I certainly hope it goes smooth with no explosions. I laugh out loud but it wasn't funny at all. I didn't hurt anyone so I push it far from my mind. I'd been divorced a year now. It was time to have a companion by my side. I miss that. I gave myself the courtesy of 'it's your turn.' We walk into the movie theater arm in arm. I smile.

CHAPTER SIX

"What's the pleasurable smile for Miss Megan?" James inquires.

"Oh, I don't know. This feels good. Hope it's a good movie!" I can't contain my excitement.

"You said you didn't like thrillers, do you want to change movies?"

Seriously, is this guy for real? He would change movies for me and go to something he wasn't into. "No. I'll take your recommendation. I'll close my eyes if it gets too bad."

"Bad as in scary?"

"Yes."

"I somehow don't take you as the scared type. I think you might like thrills." He sounds encouraging.

"You do know the ones who show no fear are the most scared of all?" I tell him something I heard my dad say once.

James looks at me contemplating this statement, then assesses me with a once over.

"You don't believe me?" I ask him.

"I do know a thing or two about nerves, nerves of steel that is."

"I believe there's quite a few things you might know about that I've yet to see."

"Possibly, but I think you've passed the fear test as in

last week." He reminds me.

I swallow. I didn't need any more reminders. "That's history."

James winks at me. I look forward and walk on in. I wasn't scared tonight with James at this movie theatre.

We sit and watch the movie. Apparently, it had been a bestselling book made into a movie. I didn't know anything about it. The last few years I couldn't read a book, only an occasional magazine article. Three boys since birth kept me more than busy. I found myself watching with exploration like I'd heard about some of these things. But how did I know about spying, intrusion, or cover-ups like in the movie? I tried to think where I'd heard about things like this. Maybe it would come to me later. The plot moves quickly and the poor gal became a raving lunatic gone mad. Hmm.

"Sounds like motherhood," I whisper with sarcasm.

"What did you say?"

"Oh nothing. Movies good."

"Popcorn?"

"Sure."

"Be right back."

I watch the movie as the protagonist walked to her car and she looked around as if someone was following her. Then she got in her car and looked to the car next to her. She saw a man looking right at her. Staring. She fiddled with her keys and started her car, backed up, and pulled away quickly. He pulled away too. She looked in her rearview mirror and he was following her. She had to stop at a light and he pulled up right beside her in the left hand lane. Dare she look over? She knew he was there. She did. He put his arm over his face to shield himself. What the hell she gasped? The light turned, she pulled away, and he was beside her. She looked again. Then he quickly turned into a parking lot across from the police station. *Was he a cop* she thought? Why was he following her? What did she do?

Someone tapped my shoulder. I jump and my nerves explode in a shiver.

"Popcorn, Megan." I recognize James's whispering voice.

"Oh, you missed a good part. Someone is following her; she doesn't know who."

I grab some popcorn and munch away.

"Good guy or bad guy?"

"Not sure," I whisper.

James put his arm around me and we finish watching this movie. I still couldn't think of where I'd heard about a few of these spying techniques. I was vaguely interested in this stuff as I'd worked for a law firm right out of business school, and they had occasionally deployed the FBI to surveil someone if one of their clients were in trouble or had become threatened.

I find myself intrigued. My interest was far removed from a normal person asking questions. I want in. I need to talk with James soon about what it is he does. I know he is not a normal cop; he seems more, more involved I say to myself. I would ask him and probe his mind for answers. Maybe this is a key to my future. What could I do? I couldn't be a cop like my dad and get shot then my boys wouldn't have a mom. I never read the book "1984." Missed that one. Maybe I should buy a copy and catch up.

Hell, I don't even watch the cop shows on television because it reminds me of death or trouble, and it brings so much pain that I just didn't want to deal with. So I don't. I listen to music instead. I was glad I discovered something outside myself-it erases the pain of my loss.

I wonder what James did to get over the death of his

dad? Maybe he confronted it head on and joined the force. But he does something else now. I just know it. He's older, too. I want to find out. He's calm. He's recovered. He's moved on. He's an adventurer. He likes thrills. I can tell.

And then it hits me as we stroll around the shopping plaza connected to the theater. I felt someone watching us just off to the side. I don't stare but notice a man pretending to be shopping or looking at items on a shelf. What?

Megan, I tell myself. *That's ridiculous*. The movie has you spellbound or something. I breathe deeper and exhale slowly. James notices.

"Thinking about the movie?"

"Yeah, do you suppose that can happen in real life?"

"Sure. But I don't think it's happening to you or me."

"How can you be so sure?"

"You would have to be connected to something or someone, for agents to be spying upon you."

I'll have to think about that. I put that thought far away and continue to enjoy our date. We stop in a casual place for a late night dinner and later drive to his place.

Once inside James and I look around and check out his house. I don't remember anything from the first date, maybe I was a bit traumatized. Now I am relaxed. I walk right over to the fireplace. Funny I hadn't seen what was on the mantle, like the picture, which was proudly displayed above. It was a photograph enlarged in full color.

"That's you! You caught a big fish?"

He walks over from the kitchen and sighs, "Yup, that's me a few years ago down in the Gulf of Mexico after a fishing trip."

"Awesome. Nice. I use to love fishing when I was a little girl. Grandma showed me how to fish. I'm pretty good you know."

"This is sounding like a possible contest of skills."

I walk over and give him a flirty wink with some drama. I pretend to cast my reel out into the ocean, drop to the bottom, lift, and wait for a bite then begin to reel in a big fish playing the part of 'it's so big it might get away.'

He smiles.

"I'll catch the biggest fish for sure."

CHAPTER SEVEN

He walks over to me and put his arms around me from behind and helps to reel in the big one. I close my eyes. I feel his body behind me. This feels nice. He holds me close for a long time. Then he turns me around and kisses me with all he has.

When our lips depart ways he says, "I'll win."

"Just like checkers. I'm betting."

"Not like checkers. I let you win, you know."

"What else are you good at?"

He looks at me quizzically.

"Oh, that sounded cheesy, huh?"

"No it didn't. Stay with me and I'll show you."

"I'd like that."

"Look over my music selection." He hands me his phone and says, "Play anything you want or just hit play for random songs."

He sets a speaker on the counter and we sip the drinks he has poured, then dance very close. I feel his arms and caress his shoulders. Damn this feels good. He puts his hands on my waist and holds me a bit tight. All these sensations I haven't felt for a year. How I've missed them. *God sure had a good plan when he made man and woman,* I thought. And I'm not even religious.

He holds out his hand and I look at the man before me with complete trust. He leads me to a room that holds cool pale colors and crisp sheets which my skin easily melts into.

The next day we pick up my boys from my ex and all of us go to the county fair. Needless to say this was the best twenty four hours I have experienced in a couple years. It just was.

The day felt natural, and yes, it was too soon for my boys to meet him. Listening to folks talk on the radio and say that you should not bring anyone into their lives until you are sure seems like good advice, as I'd listened to over this past year, but did not follow today. I found myself not thinking but acting today, acting upon what felt right. Don't think about it. Just be.

My mom would want me to be in the moment. *Don't doubt yourself Megan, she would say, you know best. I could hear her talking to me. Even though you've been burned the world is still magical. Please believe. I'm always there for you. Keep smiling. And don't ever lose your bad ass ways because I love that best about you. It makes you Megan and you make all of us women strong. My mom always wanted me to be a lawyer and stand up for others, especially women. Maybe she had a point. Maybe I should have listened to her more. I wonder if she'll like James. I think about this for a few minutes as we walk around putting the boys on the rides at the fair.* By the time the day is over we are all exhausted, and smell like the farm as we couldn't get the boys away from the animals. I'm sure we spent three hours in there.

On Sunday my boys and I sleep in very late, cook together, and watch cartoons followed by a movie. Mid-day comes and Ian suggests we should invite James to dinner. I call him and he says he would love it.

By Sunday night we make the plans for next weekend. My roommate, Alana Maria Antigua, and her child, Hope, will be back and James invites all of us out for a boat ride. School will be finished. With all the tests done, we'd celebrate Memorial Day with a picnic on his boat. "Sounds like a wonderful idea. Looking forward to it."

"See you next weekend."

"Alana, you must come with us. Please. It's just a boat ride and Hope will have fun. You both deserve some fun."

Alana Maria Antigua gives me her soft brown eyes with a twisted smile. She wants to trust me that everything will be all right, I know it, but her history tells another story. My roommate is originally from Mexico, was married, and is now divorced. Her story is long but I have befriended her and allow her to stay with me until she is able to get back on her feet. We met when we both got divorced last year. Her porcelain skin and facial features are distinct, set off by her brunette ombre` long hair. Her medium build makes her appear stronger than she actually is at the moment. And her English constantly improves while her daughters is almost perfect.

"Let me think about the boat ride." She says and then sits over on the sofa facing the window. She's pondering the event. She has been through hell so I don't push her but give her some time. I can see it reeling in her mind. Her ex-husband tried to kill her after he'd pushed her down the stairs. She wasn't dead, and he came after her to finish it when she tried to escape. It wasn't the first time he'd pushed her down the stairs. The first time she called out sick to work and her evening crew got wind of it, came to her apartment, and tried to help her. He answered the door and told them she was fine, later he beat her up pretty hard. How dare her friends try to help, he yelled at her? Then he left. She didn't know what to do. So she did nothing.

Later when she recovered she went back to work but

looked for another nursing assistant job closer to home. She missed those girls that liked her and tried to help her. They missed her, too. I look at her, she was pretty with long brown hair that in the light had Carmel streaks of light, warmth just like her. Some neighbor that overheard everything called the police, and the police actually did something. The next day he was arrested at work; she was able to leave and they put her up in a safe house. She escaped. She'd told me the whole story. She felt like the luckiest gal alive. But her story didn't end there. She had a relative who pissed somebody off, mob related, she thought. She told me she tried to figure out who might be tied to them, someone from her family but she just didn't know. Privately she confided in me that maybe her husband took money from one of his brother's arrests and they might think she knows something. She felt followed, so much, that she had become paranoid. She didn't trust the police because her ex-husband's brother was a cop and he used to tell her that he did shady deals. Complicated is what she always said. I could tell she wanted to say yes to the boat ride.

"It's just a boat ride. No one will be out there spying on any of us."

"A boat ride sounds like fun." She gave way. *Yeah,* I thought.

"Great. I want to pack a perfect picnic. What will Hope like to eat?" I ask.

"Plantains, and fruit. She loves taquitos, too."

"I'm so glad you said yes. I'll make sure we have life preservers for all of us. And you get to meet James."

"I want to meet your new guy. You seem so happy!"

"Does he have a friend?" She honestly asks.

"Ha ha. See you will have fun!"

"I'd like to make something to take."

"Salsa." I replied.

"Si, I make that. I know you love it much." I caught her smiling.

CHAPTER EIGHT

"Perfect." Hope ran into the room. She was four and quite simply the most beautiful child on this earth anyone had ever seen. She didn't seem to be bothered by her mother's situation. *Kids are so resilient* I thought. Little Hope never asked where her father was. Maybe kids are smarter than they give out. She was the light of her mother's eye, anyone could see that.

Alana told her about the boat ride out on the water and she flew around the room. "Momma, I need bathing suit."

"Si, you do."

"Let's go to the store and we'll get the groceries and a bathing suit." We pile into my van and head out. I reflect as we drive to the store. A year ago I took in, Alana Maria, and Hope, very devastated, from a halfway house, as I needed a roommate to cover the expenses and I needed another adult to balance out my own family. I had no regrets. She had just been divorced like myself. I had to swallow hard when she opened up about her past. Unbelievable. The abuse she suffered stunned me. Why would anyone treat someone so bad? I couldn't comprehend her situation but I wanted to help. I could tell she was strong, religious, and grounded but married to an asshole. But that was her past I kept telling her. She remained guarded and skeptical. I looked out for her. She used to tell me her own mother told her to stay and not leave her abusive husband. Old school I said. Your mother is old school. The saying, 'you made your bed now lie in it' came to me so many times. What is the matter with people?

"Gracias, Megan."

"For what?"

"For sticking by me and Hope. You understand me. Thank you for that."

"You deserve better. We all do."

Alana smiles. Her porcelain skin made transparent the fragility inside and I wished her happiness that she and Hope deserved. Maybe she just needs time. God's plan is what she always told me. "God will help me."

"And so will I," I reply. "You can stay with me as long as you like."

Friday morning came and after an extra hour of sleep we pack up and follow James to the marina. It was a beautiful day! Sunny with no humidity which meant in the south we could breath and not sweat the minute we walk outside like in July. Usually, I was not bothered by this situation but today I wanted to be great looking, hair and all, for me and my new guy. I had bought a new red bikini, and a cool lacy white cover-up. Even Alana thought it extra special. The boys were all packed and ready when I went to wake them this morning. Today would be fun for all.

"Hey boys, help me unload some of this gear I've brought." James asks the boys to assist him with skis, floats, and tubes. Alana, Hope, and I brought the food and coolers down the ramp to the dock. How lucky we are and in for a fine treat.

"Let me get a picture of everyone." I take a cell phone picture with the marina behind them all, boats and docks behind me, with all the kids arms piled high with our fun equipment. Off we were to a super day out on the lake.

James starts the motor and the boys help him to untie from the dock. He takes us out and speeds across the lake. The lake was quiet this morning, hardly any boats out. We have it all to ourselves until this afternoon. Lucky us!

Alana takes some pictures with her phone of Hope and the boys. We have to go slow under the bridge and our conversation echoes on the water under the bridge.

"Did you ever hear the story of the Lady of the Lake?" asks James.

"No I haven't. Please tell."

"Right here on this bridge her car went off and no one ever found her or the car until many, many years later. Quite a story. They still don't know why she went off the bridge."

"Suicide?" asks Alana.

"Not sure. Anymore guesses?"

"Drunk?" asks one of the boys.

"Maybe," replies James.

"She probably fell asleep at the wheel!" Patrick yells.

"That's a good one," I reply.

"No matter, it was years before they discovered her here. Remember ... she just disappeared. No one knew where she was." James points over to the spot where they found her car but no body, at least it wasn't reported.

"She drowned, momma," says Hope.

"Maybe there's a ghost out here on the lake waiting for us," says Ian.

"Now that's good," says James.

"Waiting for you to be the man of the lake!" Matthew hollers.

"Well, we better not let that ghost lady get us," James retorts.

As soon as we clear the bridge James speeds up again and takes us across a widened access on the lake. Nobody looked back at the bridge-nobody wanted to think about a ghost out here on the lake. We head for an inlet, a cove, he tells us. He has the boys help with anchoring. They gladly assist him to learn this feature of boating. Then it was time to swim!

We relax and pull out snacks and drinks. I have to admit this was quite relaxing.

However, when I look over at Maria she is not relaxed. She is playing with her phone and looks as though she has seen a ghost. Her face is pallid to begin with and is now drained further of living juice. She swallows, looks around with fixed eyeballs, employing a frozen stare.

"Are you okay?" I ask.

"My phone is messing up," she says.

"What do you mean?"

"Oh nothing. Must be me."

"Is Siri talking to you?" James jokes.

Alana looks up and flashes James a look of worry.

"Hey, sorry. Turn it off, then back on. Maybe you got it wet."

She turns it off then puts it down but her mood and demeanor don't go unnoticed.

Later, the boys come aboard and ask James if we can change spots. They want to go exploring on land. Alana has turned her phone back on hoping for something clearer. She still looks confused and puzzled but continues with what she is looking at.

"I've got another cove to go to where we can go on a beach. All aboard." James, our captain, keeps us all in line having a good time.

When we reach full speed I look over at Alana to see

if she is better. She looks at me, then without notice, she throws her phone overboard. I am in shock. She begins to cry and puts me off to leave her alone.

I will get to the bottom of this I tell myself. I know many times I put her off not believing all the things she told me. I thought maybe *she added items or in her post marriage state she was just stressed.* No one throws their phone overboard. Ever. Never. For now I want the day to be fun for the rest on board. This was important for the boys, and I, but I would give time to Alana. I had come to really care for her like a sister.

CHAPTER NINE

Needless to say the rest of the day is amiss. Did I miss something? I question myself. She was doing so well. Who is bothering her? Was it bad news? No because she wouldn't throw away the phone. This was troubling. I wasn't seeing something. My heart tried to reach out to her. Maybe later I would talk to James. Maybe he could help me.

Hope sits on her mommas lap. She kisses her. How sweet. I hate problems, problems that I can't solve. When we stop I go to her and touch her shoulder. I might be a busy mom but I couldn't help to think I'd missed something. She needed someone.

She and Hope go swimming with the life jackets on. I sat there for a few moments with James reveling in the pure sunshine and prettiness of the lake but preoccupied with my thoughts. It was then I told him she'd thrown her phone overboard.

"Why'd she do that? Was it broken? She'll lose all her pictures and information."

"I don't think she thought about that. That's right. All her pictures are gone."

"You should take a few of her, and Hope, she might like that."

Since Maria was enjoying herself in the water I relent

and go for a swim with James. We are able to play a little and enjoy in the newness of our brand new relationship. Relationship? Is this a relationship? I suppose if I'm asking myself that question-then quite possibly it is.

At the end of the day we load up all the equipment and head towards our vehicles. Suntan and spent from the exhilaration of a day on the lake outside in the sun made for some happy faces. James comes and asks me if he can take Alana home while I drive all the kids. I said I'll check with her and thought that a good idea. I hope he can help her and find out what's causing her troubles.

"Alana, do you mind going with James? He'll bring you home. It will give us some extra room in my car for the kids to stretch out."

"Anything for you Megan. Thanks for the boat ride and picnic James." She spoke the kind words without any emotion then put Hope in the car. Alana is a kind soul who has pulled away from the living, I think. James tells me he will get her to begin talking with him, maybe he would find out her fear.

After James drops Alana off he told me he had to run an errand. He told me she would be fine, nonetheless, phoneless for now.

"Will I see you back later?"

"Yes, I'll come back in an hour or so."

"Perfect, see you then." I want to ask the question "What did you find out?" But I held my tongue.

James point of view …

I knew what I had to do after talking with Alana Maria. I hoped I hadn't scared her. I tried not to give away what I suspected. She was being tailed through her phone but from what she told me she was also being trolled. Heavily. Poor thing was scared to death. She'd given me her number so I thought I'd go see my expert. His name was Nate. He knew everything there was to know about phones of all types. He could get into them, strip any tailing devices off of them. The only concern he would explain to me is, "James, if they are tailing you, then they are most likely covering your ass in all directions."

I drove to get some takeout food and act like I am a delivery boy. Hell, I started to have some paranoid thoughts after being around Maria for an hour. From what she told me I probably need to call some friends who have security clearance. Or better yet, I thought about making a trip to visit them. Didn't Megan say she was going to Biloxi for a few days? That's what I'll do-I'll go then and do my top secret visit. As much as I've wanted to get away from all the drama, it somehow keeps calling me back. I shake my head at my own dilemma. I had decided to settle down and open up a dive shop with an attached restaurant near the water down in the Gulf. I was thirty-three years of age and the lady at the online dating service asked me why I needed them.

"Surely, sir, you don't need any help!" she exclaimed after viewing my profile.

I replied, "Hey, you are here to help, right?"

"Yes. Yes I am." She added, "You won't be with us for long, I'm sure."

"Thanks. It's been a long time. I'm going to let you help me."

My very first date, Megan, already had given me inspiration and now I'm helping her for a friend. I turn the corner and pull into the alley, then park between two buildings out of site. I enter a small shop across the way from Le Bistro. I gave that place a second look; I should bring Megan here. She'd like that little French place I bet.

"Hello Nate, I brought you dinner."

"'Dinner and what else?"

"Let me write it down in case someone's listening." He loved it when I started talking all mysterious like James Bond or something. Nate was 27 and came from a family with government connections.

He infused that knowledge with telecommunications in addition to self-education. I believe he had a fifty-fifty contract, in other words he was self-employed and then also a part time official for the government. He knew my boss that was good enough for me.

"Hey Bear, I mean Bond," Nate said, then laughed out loud.

I join in and wrote down the make and model, followed by the question. He went and retrieved a similar phone and had it apart before I could make light conversation.

"You're not the first that's come in here. I had a client come and ask something similar. She said she felt trolled on the internet and not in a good way."

"Really?"

"Her exact words were ... can you get the bugs out of my damn phone?"

"Did she look frightened?" I ask knowing the answer.

"She looked like she had been in a room full of 'em."

I suddenly became serious; this wasn't just a troll I thought.

"I cleaned her phone and noticed the area around the camera had possibly been over heated, it had very worn areas like an acid spill. That's when I asked her if her camera had ever suddenly turned itself on?"

"What did she say?"

"She almost fainted on me dude."

"What?"

"How did you know?" she asked.

"I don't know I'm just suspecting that it's been turned on quite a lot. Did your battery wear off on you or have a short span?"

"Yes! And ... yes!"

"You've been hacked I told her."

"Then she just wanted to throw the phone against the wall. She left it here, then took off in her fancy car after she practically ran out of the place. Later she called and said I could have it-she didn't want it anymore."

"You still have it?"

"I do. Let me get it for you."

"Sounds good."

I looked around at my friend's place, he sure was a tinkerer.

"Here it is."

"Thanks. Not sure what I'll do with it yet. What's the verdict on my friend's phone?"

"Without getting to look it over, I'd say it was professionally bugged. Probably FBI, but why? I have no idea. That's your area of expertise."

"Yes, it is. But if you could have seen her face today, it was real. She was terrified."

"The real question you must ask is why are women being frightened?"

CHAPTER TEN

A nd with that I thanked my friend Nate, and left the shop. I never left Nate's without feeling more enlightened. He had that way about him. He hadn't been to school but was well schooled and he always impressed me. I trusted him with maybe too much. He was after all educated on YouTube. I put the phone in my pocket not knowing what I was going to do with some rich ladies phone.

I left the alley with thoughts of Megan on my mind and when our next date would be.

I made the decision not to discuss Alana Maria's mess with Megan, thinking this would just make things worse. I needed to find out more about Maria's past and this other lady, who had similar situations. Megan seemed to be a bystander, as in her roommate, I was not concerned for her safety unless someone saw us on our first date.

Megan's point of view …

James finally returns and for that I was thankful. The kids had retreated earlier to their rooms supposedly watching a movie; I knew they wouldn't last long from being in the sun all day and playing in the water. You could always trust Mother Nature to whip her little chittlins good just when their flesh and blood, human mother, needed a break. I didn't need a total break I wanted a break to spend more time with James, my new guy. And I want to find out what he thought about Maria.

"Everybody in bed already?" he asks. The sun on his tan skin only made him more appealing.

"In bed, streaming a movie."

He smiles and winks at me. What?

"How about we watch a movie on the sofa?"

"Let me find one."

"Maria okay?" He asks.

"She seems fine. She turned in when Hope fell asleep. I think she is reading and not missing her phone at all."

"Phones. You have any issues with yours?" he asks.

I could tell there was a concern and I answer. "No, never."

"Good. Perfect. Let's enjoy a movie and forget about them for a while."

I don't hesitate and join James on the couch. Feeling like a girl in high school about to be making out soon gave me a thrill, the good kind that is.

"Eat, Pray, Love," he said. "I never saw this have you?"

"This might be my fourth time, ha ha!"

James then pulls me close and we kiss. Oh, how I was falling for this man before me. But should I? Maybe it was too late. When he stops I reach back and hold his face so I could hold on and kiss him again. Then I settle back into him and watch Julia Roberts on the screen. *I have no worries* I think to myself.

James reaches for the remote and pauses the movie. "Before we get further involved I want to ask you to go on a date with me, a special date?"

"Sure, when?"

"Before I go out of town on business a week from this Monday. I'll be gone for a week then."

"What's special about the date?" I ask.

"I'd like to take you to a special place I think you'll like, no kids, just you and I."

"I'm listening. Where is this place?"

"It's in Roswell, off the beaten path, in this cozy little street of boutique bars and restaurants. I think you'll like it."

"I'd love to. I'll wear a nice dress, get fixed up for a romantic date!"

"Perfect. Great."

He starts the movie again and we both lay there a bit dreamy, cozy, and unaware that the phone James laid high up on a shelf above us suddenly turns on.

The next morning James leaves before anyone is awake, and unlike him, he forgot the phone. Maybe he'd had such a good day, and night, with the family he forgot what he was trained to do for so many years. I found it when I made my morning coffee and set it back on the shelf. I would call him later to let him know where it was. All this fuss over phones. Unbelievable.

I knew one thing he couldn't wait for next Saturday night and neither could I. He told me as much right before we fell asleep. I made a note to go shopping for something special to wear.

"Morning Alana," I said as she walks into the kitchen. She looks at me and shakes her head up and down with a tiny smug smile lined by a closed mouth. Not the typical greeting she usually gave me, but more like she had something on her mind. Maybe she is just happy for me.

I put my arm around her and told her everything would be okay. "James even said things will be all right. Do you believe us?"

"I don't know. Maybe I'll move back in with my mother."

"But you don't really like your mother; she doesn't like you. You told me that."

"I know," She shook her head back and forth. "But I can't be a burden to you forever."

"Alana Maria, let me check into apartments or roommate rentals for you. Nursing school takes up much of your time and little Hope still needs you, at least until she gets into 1st grade. Give me a couple weeks, okay?"

Her eyes want to see a glimmer of hope but she just stares at me and I am lost. I want to help more but I have my three guys and I need to move my life forward, too.

Just then we hear a ruckus of sorts and both of us head to the front door. The kids have answered the door and a man is asking them questions. He is large and round. He's asking about an exercise bike.

"What? What's going on?" I ask.

He steps right past the kids and enters my home moving around looking at rooms. We all just stare. What is he doing? I'm growing worried with each second and usher the kids to the hallway to go upstairs.

He explains. "I'm looking for the seller of an exercise bike."

"We don't have one." I stand up right next to him, not sure whether I could maneuver him or get him to leave. He pauses and takes one more look around. *What the hell* I think? He is in my front hallway uninvited circling around looking at and in all the rooms.

He stares at me and I want him gone.

Everyone else has gone upstairs.

"I must have the wrong house."

Damn right I think. Get the hell out of my house. I have no idea what I would do but he just entered my house uninvited, and frankly, I was rather disgusted at his intrusion. And he stared at my kids for a long time. I slam the door as he steps over the threshold, then lock it.

Alana stares at me with pleading eyes. I can't really give her any comfort as I am instantly torn up by this intrusion. Disgustingly bold and who was he anyway? My heart begins to beat fast. I just didn't know. What should I do? Calm down Megan. Be in charge. *Fuck it.*

I look around and back at Maria. She needs my strength. I must give it to her.

"I don't know what he wanted. Wrong house, that's all," I spoke. I didn't believe a word I said. Strange. *Motherfucker.*

CHAPTER ELEVEN

The phone rang and the kids pick it up. "Mother, it's for you. It's your boyfriend!" I hear giggles. Kids bring you right back into reality. That shook me out of any uncertainty I was feeling.

"Hello."

"Megan, I'm thinking about you and I miss you."

"James, how sweet of you. I had a great weekend."

"Me too."

"I miss you."

"I want to confirm our date next Saturday. Are we on?"

"Yes, I'm going to confirm with Alana. I think she'll be here another week. I'm going to look for a place for her to stay. She needs some assistance for another year then little Hope will be in school; she'll have her Associates of Science Degree in Nursing and can get a better job to support them both."

"Ah yes, it's friendly of you to help her this past year. I know she appreciates the support."

"Thanks. I try."

"Oh, I almost forgot. I left a friends phone in your house. Have you found an extra one?"

"Yes. I did find it."

"I'll stop over at the end of the day to pick it up."

"Sure, bye."

"See you later."

Mid-morning already but I head to my computer to check my emails. Lots of stuff here which I mostly delete. In the middle of all the garbage is one from an old college roommate. She works for the government and wants me to write an article for a monthly magazine about my divorce. She says it will help others to know how I got through it. They'll pay me $75 and if I speak at a luncheon that's another $225. This sounds like easy money-so I reply sure let me know the dates. She immediately replies back that we'll need to meet for coffee, or lunch, whichever one I prefer. I say sure and we schedule a quick coffee for tomorrow morning. I pay the bills then it's time for a quick workout, followed by kids swim lessons, lunches, and afternoon camp for the older one, a nap or movie for the younger two, pickups, then dinner.

Days go fast with the boys. But I consider myself lucky to be off for the summer. I know eventually I will have to be at work year round, but for now I had enough to support all of us through alimony and child support. It helps that my ex's parents have extra and adore their grandkids. They will take them for the month of July. Sweet for me. I was the big momma for the month of June. *Bring it on* I told myself!

Saturday arrives and Alana assures me she will love to watch all the kids and told me to sleep over and come home Sunday. I smile. *Now there's a woman on my side* I thought. I hope she will start dating and get a personal life, if only for a few hours for herself. I told her this and she shrugs it off then finally says, "Okay, maybe Miss Megan."

I need to convince her to stay with me. I tell her I think we could help each other watching each other's kids like we have been doing for a year now. We were a perfect fit, both young parents in need of that back up spouse that neither of us has at the moment. True, I was searching more than her. *Life had been tougher on her* I thought. She needed more time to trust again. I was beginning to think I was ready.

I put on a new dress I bought, a flowy bottom half with extra swirl and a beaded top half with a streamlined bodice. I thought it fit perfect in all the right places. Comfortable, yet it had a sexy look. The color was dark brown not my usual pick but with the tan I was acquiring my skin seemed to glow more than usual. Definitely "sexy" is what I tell myself when I look into the mirror!

James arrives and the boys go out to greet him. He talks with them and shows them his fancy sports car. He tells them he's just cleaned it and they can climb in it later or another time as its ready for me. He wants it to be perfect for our date. He's looking at me through the front door.

The boys run back to get me and tell me to have a good time. I assure them I will and tell them to follow Miss Alana's instructions. The boys watch me get into the car-I think they may be jealous.

James looks at me after we are belted in and asks, "Ready dear?"

"Am I ready for the fifth round?"

"Counting are we?"

"Dates, yes."

"Am I doing well?"

"Just making sure we don't repeat the first one."

"That was a once in a lifetime event Miss Megan."

"I'm not so sure James."

"I am fairly certain I won't be able to top that one. Trust me."

James said we were going to a French bistro.

"Sounds marvelous, though, I don't have a clue what to

order. Do you?"

"My dear I spent a good time traveling in my past life, so yes, I can order for us. I think the menu though is in English, so no worries."

James sped off with a quick push to the pedal. We are locked in and on our way. The music is playing and we are off to the French Bistro. I think to myself that I'm very glad I did not wait to begin dating again. This thought makes me smile. I'm in a good place.

When we stop for gas I take a selfie in James's car. I just had to. We smile and make a couple of cheesy looks. We make light chatter when I notice how awesome he smells. This makes me feel great. How long has it been to be sitting next to a man? I made the decision right there driving in his car I would not miss out anymore, even if we didn't work out.

I send the selfie to a couple friends. I laugh. Now they would know I was dating and I would get a hundred questions. Better not send it to my family as yet. I certainly didn't want a lecture about getting involved, or when was I getting married? James turns up the music in the car and we sit there a few more moments, then he turns back out to the highway.

Undecidedly our emotions are up in the clouds and we just enjoy the ride.

Once off the highway he pulls down side street after side street and I have no idea where I am. Then down an alley he parks between two buildings. I look over at him.

"It's my own little spot, reserved just for us."

The magic of the night has just swooped in.

CHAPTER TWELVE

"For you, Madame."

The host seats me first in a small little room just off the upstairs main room. I determine it's an old house or store from the 1800's or something like that. It has wooden floors and walls with pictures, black and white, bicycles, beaches, and faraway places. The mood is definitely romantic. Soft music plays in the background while our wine is delivered. James and I sit side by side. There's even a mirror over on the hand painted wall by the window.

"No explosions tonight, please."

"None."

"Have you found out anything from the incident? Anything you can tell me?"

"I will find out next week as I'm going to a meeting for a few days."

"Are you? Can you tell me where?"

"No I cannot. I will tell you when I can, just not yet."

"Okay, I'll trust that for now."

"How about your coffee? Anything turn up from that?"

"Yes. I'll be going away for a couple days myself."

"Good, then we'll both be gone. Nothing to miss out on."

"I'm changing the subject. Why do you want to move

to the coast?"

"Did I tell you that? Or was that on the dating site?"

"The dating site."

"I've wanted to live near the coast my whole life, ever since I was a kid and we lived one house away from the lake. Every day is different and you know the temperament of the lake is how the day is faring."

"Yeah."

"I may sound misguided but it's true. I feel landlocked if I'm not near the water-though, I love the pines of Georgia and the mountains to the north, there's a personality of the lake or ocean that changes and that is what I love."

I sat there listening and knew exactly what he was talking about and it sure sounded like poetry coming out of his mouth. I'd like to feel what he was expressing. It got me thinking what did I feel about the land? Frankly, I didn't know. I had never listened to nature like he was describing. I know this is when I fell in love with James. It happened in that moment and I was changed.

"Megan," he said. I look at him.

"Yes?"

"Have you ever been there?"

"Yes, I went to the ocean as a kid with my parents. I had a blast. I wasn't scared of sharks. I grew up near the lake in Ohio and swam in the waters."

"You must come back to the sea with me."

"Mr. Hemingway, I'd love to. When?"

"Soon in fact. First up, though, I just found out I have a house on Lake Lanier for three weeks in June and July. I'd like you and the boys to come, it will be fun."

"Let me think. Their camps will be done after next week so that may work."

"What about the swim lessons?"

"All done by then. My in-laws will take them the month of July right after the fourth."

"So you'll come? For three weeks? And maybe the boys can come for a week before they go to the in-laws?"

"I'm pretty certain we can do that. Let me ask them. Alana still seems a bit creeped out from her phone she threw overboard."

"Is she on the internet at all at your house?"

"Not too much, she's been reading books and studying for school as she's in summer school at the Tech College."

"Most likely trolls are bothering her."

"We did have a visitor one day last week."

"A visitor?"

"Yes, very creepy indeed."

"Why is that?"

"I don't know. I actually forgot about it. Let's forget about it. Too weird."

James looks at me and I could tell his brain was deciphering this last bit of information but I blow it off when our food arrives. I wasn't sure what he ordered for us but it looks fantastic.

Our dinner is cozy and every bit romantic as we take our time savoring all these flavors from the French cooking. We share a few intimate details and tease each other from time to time. This night is perfect thus far. I hope it stays that way. Our cocktails make it through the meat course and we skip dessert. Instead we go for a walk, up and down the street, looking and watching other people enjoy the evening. It is a nice night, no chill, no heat, just right.

On the way home to his place we lay out the plans for the month of June, as we are just a few weeks into our dating. We would both be gone on trips at the same time, return, then off to the lake house for three glorious weeks.

How could I turn down a place at the lake for three weeks, and free at that? I couldn't I determine and the boys would love it I was sure, even if for just for a few days. This man I had just met seems to be the one, dare I say that? One little thing-he was going to move to the beach next year he told me. And what did he exactly do for work? That was still hanging out to dry. In other words I had no idea who this man really was. Should I look him up? My friend told me a way to search someone and get the goods on them via the internet. Maybe that wasn't such a bad idea. I could call the dating service and ask them.

We couldn't even wait once the front door was shut. I had eaten my first French dinner and I was even more ravished than before. *Save me James from myself* I thought.

CHAPTER THIRTEEN

The next day we decide to go for a walk in the park, not before I see a couple guys in a truck outside my front lawn near the curb. They were fixing or playing with some wires out front. One guy was big with no distinguishable clothing apparel on. They weren't from the phone company or internet server. Just an old truck with two guys riding shotgun. That struck me as bazaar. How many other houses wires were they working on? *What's up with your mind Megan* I ask myself? Listening to your roommate too much? You don't even believe her. You want to but you don't. Slowly, though, I was being dragged into the net.

"Megan, what do you think about that? Thoughts?" I was in my own thoughts and missed James entire question directed at me.

"Sorry, I missed it. What did you say?" I ask.

"I asked you what career you might be pursuing. You said you wanted to work when all the boys went to elementary school which will be this fall."

"I did say that, didn't I?"

"So you're not sure yet."

"I did some business for a law firm and they liked me a lot. But sixty hours I cannot do with three boys and a mother who lives four states away. I have a medical background in that I took courses relatable along with business. "

"You want 30-40 hours, correct?"

"Thirty sounds good, that way I can be a mom for ten plus per week."

"Ten hours of your undivided attention with things like reading, sports, playing, cooking, and bath time fun!" James winks at me.

"Being a mom is 24/7 but people either have to work because they need the money or they want to work because a mom at home has very little relief. And it's tough being a commando 24/7 times 18 years."

"You are looking for balance. I get it."

"How are you so understanding? You don't even have kids?"

"Because I had a mom who gave me attention and love and later when she went to work she reserved time for me. Much later on the boys and I only wanted her for dinner. When we were sick, though, she waited on me and nursed me back to health with love and kindness in addition to her smiles."

"Oh my goodness, you were a momma's boy!"

"Aren't we all?"

"Some of us are daddy's girls," I respond. "Some of us want to be just like dad, all powerful and knowing and ruthless."

"I can see that, definitely. You have that courage that you show those around you." James says and stares at me a little longer than usual.

"I didn't mean the ruthless part. I just added that for power, for guts. I don't think I want to be on the other end of your ruthlessness, your finesse. Back to the job talk. I want to help other people who can't help themselves. Maybe I should work in healthcare or for a nonprofit."

"That's an idea. You have a Business Associates Degree, right?""

"Yes, I do, and I've worked with the law office. There's my lifeguard work, too. Now, I'm a mom of three, single and looking for work this fall."

He smiles at me.

"What? I probably went to the dating site too soon, right?" I ask him this sincerely. I was wondering this myself, but here I was falling in love, all over again.

"The right time ... you went at the right time." He stops me on our walk in the park and turns me to kiss him. Before I close my eyes I study his face and revel in the name of love. How beautiful. Nothing matters, only him. I should sell this new feeling across the entire internet. I'd be a billionaire. *What an idea?* I laugh.

"Tell me what's so funny?'

"Ha ha. I'm solving the world's problems bringing peace to those who have none."

"I'll help you. Sign me up."

When we approach our car I look back at the nearby park bench. That's odd, there's that guy from the back of the old pickup truck, the very one messing with wires near my home. What the hell? Should I tell James? Must be nothing. *Megan, get a hold of yourself* I tell myself.

Back at my house, I check my computer for emails and such, and quickly browse my Social Medias. When to my surprise I see a picture that looks like a park with wires and a man on a park bench. Ha. Funny. That's the scene I just saw. Guess my internet is trying to make me feel bugged. Thanks internet for being: smarter than me, following me, and literally trying to maneuver, into every aspect of my life. The real question was who was trying to frighten me and for what reason? I wasn't born yesterday, after all my dad worked intelligence before he died in a plane hijacking accident. Or was it a plane accident my mom used to ask? He also did police work for a time. I was fully aware that I seemed a little paranoid, but under the circumstances I allowed myself the gift of knowledge. It was entirely possible, and I wasn't going to give away how scared I was underneath. I was tough, really tough. *You want to play rough* I thought? It takes two to tango. I'd never been to Paris but now that I had just fallen in love I thought why not?

I invite James to stay for a pizza night. We sit out back on the deck with lit candles, fresh air, and the half-moon in the back ground.

We plan our June-July schedule and feel a peaceful excitement about the future. Even with Maria going a bit crazy, the explosion on our first date, and each of us with our own secrets the summer love affair was heading into full gear. There was no stopping this train we had both stepped onto. We had no idea at that moment what ride we were both in for. Not a clue. Not one. Innocence like a young deer chomping on leaves in someone's back yard.

"I think Maria has me questioning too many strange occurrences," I say.

"Maybe she just has you getting up to speed," he replies.

Stunned. I look at him with one eye cocked up under the raised eyebrow. "What?"

"You heard me. She has you questioning things that should be questioned."

"I'm listening." I relent.

"Listen to your inner instincts."

"Here I was going to call her crazy but hesitated knowing she might react worse than throwing her phone into the water."

"Sometimes the people telling a story that no one is

listening to are actually telling the truth." James laid it all out with one flat honest statement.

"Pizza is here. Mom, pizza!" Ian yells.

I'm out of time to evaluate what James just said to me, so I'll have to think about it later. I look out over my yard, up to my house with windows, and over to the neighbors. Maybe I wasn't paranoid, I knew I wasn't, but I didn't have explanations for the things that I was experiencing. It had to be Maria, or maybe something my dad did a long time ago. Then again maybe my brother was into something I didn't know about. Who was James anyway? He needs to come clean and he said he would after his trip next week. And he should tell me about the 19,840 dollars we confiscated given out between rascals in the bar. Relax Megan, next week you will know everything you super sleuth!

I go inside to get plates and napkins and turn on some music.

We have a pizza party under a half lit moon and a sky full of stars. Yeah, I was beginning to feel on cloud nine all the time.

CHAPTER FOURTEEN

I open my eyes and find myself staring at the ceiling. Just like that out of the blue. What a perfect evening I'd had with everyone out back, even Maria and Hope joined us for pizza. I love May, June too, right before July opened the door to its annual sauna experience. I don't know why I decide to rise out of bed and walk to the front of the house. But I do.

Even the moon was low now but it gave some light as I look out the front window. Marias car was driving right across my visual line. Or was it her car? I blink and stare hard, just long enough to know it was her. I saw her silhouette. She didn't tell me she had a middle of the night appointment. Maybe she was flying out of the airport, and, therefore, going to the airport super early. I shook my head. I didn't like this. No need to wake up James who was sleeping in another room with the boys. I tiptoe to Maria's room and carefully open the door. I didn't want to wake up Hope. I saw that Hope was fast asleep clutching her girl doll with long hair. Maria's bed was empty, messy, and empty. It was her. But why?

The next thing I knew I found myself driving but where on earth was I going? The time was three am. I had glanced at the lap top on her bed and had seen an email open to a male name with her last name. Must be her brother. She was going to meet her brother. I read the email and it said "not the quarry but the marble house. Remember when we were kids and we played there?"

I set my phone to the only marble place I knew in all of north Georgia. Seriously, Maria, in the middle of the night? What am I doing? I really don't know except that I'm acting like some bat out of hell racing to help my roommate.

There's no one on the road, it's black but the lines are lit up well. I probably should have woke James but then the kids would ask too many questions. I also needed someone to stay and watch the house and kids. Her long lost brother is reaching out to her. How wonderful! Maybe he's undercover and can't meet her in the daylight. I slap my thigh, then slap my face. *Get a grip* Megan, *grow up*. I turn on the radio loud enough to hear but low enough to get my directions.

Before long, and after every thought I could conceive of why she is meeting her brother at an old marble house, I'm here and I recognize the big old Iron Gate-except it looks abandoned and ominous. Tall weeds are all around it on both sides. I open it, then get back in the car and pull forward, and then out again to close it back up. What am I doing? I realize I should probably have left my car down the road. I'm in. Let me find her. I follow the old road that winds all around the property. I thought somebody bought the old marble place; I guess they did but haven't done anything or opened it as yet. I remember I came here as a kid for a special Thanksgiving dinner.

"Megan," I tell myself out loud, "find Maria. Maybe you should call her cell." That's when I hear a scream. "Oh no." I get back in the car and go even slower to not be noticed but follow towards the shrill.

My heart quickens. My breath is silent in fear. I stop my

car just around the first turn inside the gate but still close to it. I wait. Should I do this? My skin tightens and the goosey flesh reminds me this is not normal. Danger. But what kind? The road travels to the right and beyond looks like a barn and the old big place, then to the left is an old shack close by the river. I park over to the left of the wooden shack and get out quietly because the scream seems to have come from this spot. I look around in the dark-she must be in that old building.

I walk closer to the river-I see that Maria's car is pulled in among the tall weeds. No Maria. I don't know what to do at this point. I'm not trained for spying or sleuthing and now my hands are practically drenched but my mind says go forward. Why was someone screaming?

I walk into the direction of the scream. It has been maybe ten minutes since the scream. I am scared but proceed to find out what is going on. Why am I doing this?

Meanwhile, earlier, Maria's dilemma and interlude...

Maria found the old storage house down by the river. She and her brother used to play here as kids. He picked a good spot for them to meet. She was so glad he emailed her even if it was so late. She would do anything for him. He was a good kid and she missed him! She came to the door and saw a candle was lit inside, actually, a few candles. The glass was broken on the door but the door knob still turned. She was using the moonlight to open the door. She caught herself smiling. She couldn't wait to give him a big hug.

"Angel, I'm here."

When her eyes became adjusted to the lower light inside she looked across the barren and dusty room to see two persons in chairs, tied to them, and heads bowed. She screamed. And she ran to them.

She touched one of them searching for Angel, going

from one back to the other. Bloody and lifeless, she gasped. Their arms were chilled and when she felt them again she lost her footing and became lightheaded losing her balance. She fell.

Someone offered her water to drink, how nice. Then she fell back asleep.

When she awoke she found herself tied to a chair facing the other two and a woman with red hair between them. Maria focused her eyes shaking her head and felt queasy. She is going to vomit. What stops her is the site of the red haired woman. Where has she seen her? She can barely think. Her stomach wretches and heaves while her throat strains letting her bulging eyes scour the face of the red headed woman. Her eyes focus with a sickening blur followed by a wet glaze.

Just then her cell phone goes off and buzzes in the front pocket of her jean jacket. Megan had given her a cell phone to borrow and only a couple people knew her number.

"What's this?" The tyrannical wretched voice came right in front of her and the frozen eyes of ice glued themselves to Maria. What was going on? Maria felt panicked and defenseless. She knew in that moment her life was going to end. But why? The voice from hell picked the phone out of her pocket, then laughed, then smacked Maria across the face as her ring sliced a wound five inches long. "Four victims in one night-I guess it's my lucky night."

Maria tries repeatedly to focus on the woman in front of her. Warm oodles of blood begin pouring down her cheek and drip from her chin. She's tied so she cannot wipe the life dripping onto her chest and clothes. It hits the phone. Maria's own voice hits her with the line of fire, her questions.

"Where's my brother? What did you do? Did you kill him?"

"Oh dear, too many questions. You're not an agent and

I need to finish what I started."

Maria saw her in the light and for some reason took notice. Was this a glimmer she might make it out of here? Not likely. Nonetheless, Maria was not herself. For some reason the panic she felt moments ago stirred an energy she didn't know existed. The fact that her phone was ringing meant someone knew she had left and maybe was coming to get her. Save her. She decided to ask this bitch some questions and turn the table on her. *It's what Megan would do in this instance* she told herself.

Long, dark red burgundy hair with fits of orange flowed over her left shoulder and down the side onto an outfit. Her right sided locks were swept up and over to the back. She wore a costume with sequins. And her lips were drawn with a smoky black burgundy lipstick in perfect measurement. Sequins trailed around a bustier with spaghetti straps holding up her cleavage and crossing in the back. Tight black leather pants kept in a body that worked out. Maria would be no match for this badass but she kept on noticing and asking a few questions about her.

"You have a name?"

"Don't worry you're not getting out of here to tell anyone. But sure they call me Rebekka."

"Rebekka, or maybe Darjeeling Red." Why Maria said that she didn't know?

"My, we are full of it, hey?" She paused to think about that, then turned to Maria with a knife and put it to her cheek opposite the side she already disfigured. Maria stared unafraid and Rebekka took notice. "Bekka for short and I don't drink tea you little shit."

"Bekka the bat, like the way you are flying around here all crazy." Maria said in her best English.

"I want you to know what's going to happen to you and

what happened to the others in here tonight. Do you see they were living and now are gone forever? Never to distract me again or endanger my life."

"They hurt you?"

"Did they hurt me?" She walked away and went over to their lifeless bodies. "Each one has crossed the line."

"You caught them sleeping with your man?"

Rebekka turned and Maria saw her eyes, black and still, a sign of a cold and empty life. For a moment Bekka stopped and waited like she was thinking.

"Never mind. You mean nothing to me."

"You have familia?" Maria has little time and she knows it.

"Oh, honey, do I have familia? What are you a border crossing, or didn't go to school?"

"Learning all the time," she replied with calmness in light of the magnitude of fear in the room.

"Let me school you. I'm in charge here and I do have family, a twin by the way that looks just like me. Identical. Put that in your pipe and smoke it!"

"Where is she? She probably needs to know you will be all right."

"She's long gone. Ever heard of Jekyll and Hyde? That's us. You got the Hyde tonight baby. How lucky you are." Rebekka laughed on and on crazy like.

Maria listened and didn't know what to say. She froze.

"You don't have any idea of who I am, do you?" Asked the maniacal women thrust before poor Maria.

"Should I?" Maria acted bold and not caring because she knew her life was over. She was going to fight for it with every last ounce of energy that directed her own blood flow.

"Let's just say I know Mickey and Joe. Ring a bell asshole?"

"Joe as in my Joe? What's my ex got to do with you?"

"Your ex is my man now, except he's bothered by your missing brother. I'm taking care of that since you are the only one he'll ever contact."

"You shouldn't be with those guys! They are bad guys."

Rebekka came at Maria and sucker punched her hard.

"Bitch."

She screamed but nothing came out. Gasping for air she knew she didn't have long. Keep her talking, wasting more time. That's what she needed. Time. She murmured through the pain. "Where did Joe find you, out on the streets?"

"You know too much. You are a loser that's why Mickey beat you up."

"And he hasn't laid a hand on you?"

Rebekka paced the floor, and circled around her first two victims, sitting there bludgeoned to death. Then she walked over to the slabs of marble, cold just like her, and picked up one of two long swords. The relic was from the civil war and her new boyfriend would be very proud; she'd overheard him say that he had put a couple of those in safe keeping. She'd found them and brought them with her tonight. This was her night, her deal.

Just then the phone rang again. Rebekka picked up the phone, walked it over to her specimen and demanded the code. "Do it. Open it."

Maria decided she needed to open it to defer the inevitable. Immediately she saw it was from Megan. She opened the lock then Rebekka hurriedly snatched it as it opened.

A whistling began ... Rebekka turned up the volume. The whistling was a song, "Oh, I wish I was in the land of cotton, old times there are not forgotten, look away, look away, look away Dixieland."

It replayed again.

There in the corner stood a tall blonde haired Megan and she had a sword in her hand. My God it had been years since she held a sword but her daddy had taught her well and there she stood in place. Not a second at hand to think about an outcome. Prominence he had taught her underscores any hesitation by the other side.

CHAPTER FIFTEEN

Megan's point of view …

Rebekka replays the message, more to bide her a moment of time. She didn't appear scared, no, rather she was like a spider securing its prey. This was going to be fun. I could tell she was happy to see me, another life to expunge from her site. Her score would be four or so she thought.

"Hey you over there, you been watching from outside?" Rebekka taunts me right away.

I remain silent eyeing my villain.

"You know Mickey, her ex?"

"Megan, she's serious. Be careful."

"That's right Megan, be careful. You don't know who you are playing with."

"I don't play games. You been tailing Maria, scaring her, trolling her, haven't you?"

"Whoa. She catches on quick." Rebekka sequestered her sarcasm.

"You're dating her ex, a no good, and decide to bully, rather murder, who gets in your way."

"Let's cut the talk and get it on."

"Let's do it. I've got my weapon." I had no time to think but from watching outside I knew there to be two swords. I found the other one after I came through the door as I rang the phone I'd lent Maria. As soon as it played my Dixie tune I knew time was up.

I wish I had time to call James but I didn't. It was then I realize I'm in my nightclothes. I stood there in boots with a jean jacket on. I look at my opponent, dressed like a Goddess of the night or from some medieval battle, ready to fight. She definitely gets the Steam-Punk Queen Title in my book.

"Hold on Maria, I'll get you out of here."

With that Rebekka lets out a tremendous, thundering laugh, which sounds like she is high on drugs. Startled but not distracted I take aim and launch my attack. I approach her and think I will go for the middle. Maria sits and watches our silhouettes piercing one another by flicker of candlelight. The dance begins as a duel between us strangers for an unknown purpose. I only know what I came upon. There are two dead people strapped in chairs, and Maria, my roommate, is still alive. Rebekka, ready to kill more tonight is delighted that I have joined the battle. It's possible that no one would find their way out of here, certainly not the two already dead.

Rebekka starts rambling on. Is she scared of my unknown abilities? I wonder. I let her ramble while I scope the situation more visibly.

"Miss Megan with the ancient sword from the civil war who likes to play music has met more than her match. Mickey and I duel all the time, especially these past six months. He's taught me well. You should drop the sword before you begin. So much blood will be shed, my darling."

A moment of silence.

"He lets me fantasize and go for the kill. But he knows I'm actually stronger than him and would really win."

I want to say is that right? But I don't. I keep letting her talk. Maybe she'll give out more info.

"I will rule his heart, mind, and he'll be mine forever. Just like it should be."

She continued on, "He told me he would revenge the things done wrong to me." She laughs and appears giddy.

"This is my lucky night. I'll get the revenge and be a hero to him."

This unfolding drama is not what I expected when I left the house. Why didn't I call James to alert him? Cops should be here, not me, handling this evil woman who is deranged. *No more time to think Megan,* I tell myself. You followed your friend and now you need to save her, and yourself. That was the bottom line.

I know if James had a clue he would come right away. I say a quick prayer for him to come, and then, I let go some hidden anger inside me to defend us both.

Right in front of Maria, Rebekka trips me, and I fall to the ground while Rebekka seizes the opportunity to make one final blow. She aims for my heart with one long drawn perilous move. But before her sword can strike a gunshot goes off. Silence. Then smoke clouds the gun from the doorway and gives way to the killer as the assailant Rebekka is hit dead on. Rebekka freezes in her stance, her forehead bloody from a single shot, and for a split second seems to gaze in the direction of the bullet. Who drew a gun on her? I had no idea. But I close my eyes as she falls over to my left side while I turn to my right. The sword falls between us.

Quickly, I get up and wonder who is here. I see two men and their shadows coming through the door. It's James, followed by Maria's ex, Mickey. Mickey is holding the gun still with both hands. I cannot believe James is walking towards me. I cannot believe I am not dead. I take a deep breath and exhale this traumatic episode, knowing, for now it has ended better than it could have.

I ask James how he found me. He says he made it to the gate after he called Nate to see if he knew where Maria went. Nate told him she was at some marble house near the river. What was going on he wondered? No one lived here anymore, worked here, or made use of the place for years now. He looked around and opened the Iron Gate. It had been a beautiful night. Now what happened? The gate door swung open and he drove his car through. He didn't bother to shut it because he was going to get the girls, me and Maria, then leave quickly. But why were you here he kept asking?

He says he drove too fast across a faint old drive and headed for the river. He saw a glimmer of light coming from an old building near the river. He stopped ahead of time and pulled his gun from the glove compartment. I didn't know he carried a gun, he didn't want to scare me he says so he hadn't shown it to me as yet. Now seemed like a good time out here in an abandoned, secluded area.

As he got closer to the building his senses geared up he said. Something was amiss. Something foul he could smell it. He heard metal on metal. Quickly and quietly he went to the window from where the metal slicing was coming and peered in the old building. He saw two female bodies dueling. What the hell he thought as he spied myself in my night clothes with a sword in my right hand? Then he saw her facing them. From the back it looked like Maria. Her head moved with the bodies exploding upon one another. Good. She was still alive. He tells me all of this rather quickly.

He couldn't see behind them what waited for him as he baited his time to enter from the glassless door beyond. Without a sound he went to the open door and slid in unnoticed.

James looked upon the dueling women. He described the duel and sparring as a fight among accomplished athletes, except their faces showed the zealous fight to be much more!

James explains that Nate had called the cops earlier than he said he would. Two more came through the door and began to guard the area.

"Don't shoot." I put my hand in the air, while the other held a sword. The cop approaches me slowly and asks for the sword. I lay it down. "Why are you here?"

"I got a call, an anonymous tip."

"I'm glad you are here."

Maria focuses her eyes and breathes shallowly then closes her lids. She quietly faints while sitting in the chair.

I look over at her and go to her. "She's fainted; we must lay her down."

The police officer looks over at the other two bodies in the chairs.

"Quickly." I plead.

"Yes, let me help." The officer responds to this bloody scene in shock himself.

I look up at him and recognize him. "You're Maria's ex."

"Yes, I am."

I pause.

"You piece of shit just saved my life?" I whisper.

We lower her down to the ground and I check her breathing, using my lifeguard skills, while I keep talking to her.

When Maria wakes she closes her eyes again and shakes her head. She was too weak at first to talk but later recovers. James assists us while the other policemen take control of the murder scene. Three dead women, two victims, and one perpetrator, but why is the question both are asking?

James and I are questioned first and then Maria. Maria has questions for her ex, like why was he here after tormenting her for weeks now? He said he wasn't tormenting her-she told him his girlfriend admitted to it.

"We've been dating for about six months, that's all. I swear." Mickey explains. Mickey is stunned, I can tell. He has just shot this woman dead, unknowingly, it is his girlfriend. "What you think-I put her up to this? No way."

The investigator arrives on the scene and begins asking more questions.

Maria persists with very little energy left. "I think you should ask him. I think he knows something. She said you keep trying to find out where my brother is, that is your total focus. She emailed me to come here tonight, and I did thinking my brother Angel was going to be here. I'd like to see him. That's why I came."

"Your brother is a wanted man. That's why I try to keep finding him. Rebekka must have figured out a way to lure you here. I was not behind that."

"You're the bad guy, even though you're a cop," issued Maria. "Who let you be a cop anyway?"

Mickey turned his head. "My brother Joe got me on board. I know I did you wrong but that was then and I'm different now. I am."

"I can't forget about it. You almost killed me."

"I know women can't forget but I don't have a record and I've done well."

"You don't have a record because that brother of yours let you go, got it switched, torn up or thrown out. Crooked."

"I know all of that is true and I'm sorry. Really, I am."

"Sorry doesn't cut it. Adios."

"I think I did the right thing tonight. I think Joe would be proud of me for saving your friend's life."

"Yes, you did save her life. Bien."

"I know I might not be able to stay on the force but I am sorry for what I did to you. I was an animal and evil back then."

I look at him. I look at Maria. Maria looked at him. She's contemplating his words. She looks exhausted.

"Maria is tired and confused with almost losing her life, mine too. Let's leave it at that, you did save our lives tonight." I say.

The other cop comes over with a bottle of liquid and shows it to the investigator. "You can probably guess what this is?"

"Liquid Xanax," replies the investigator.

Maria hears that and tells him, "I think she drugged me … I don't remember how she tied me … up in the chair She did give me a drink of water after I saw the dead victims." He listens to her and takes his notes by phone recording her words.

"The water must have been the liquid Xanax." I add.

After I gave my statements I turn my head side to side and look at James. "What a mess."

I begin to shake and shiver in the middle of the night in early June in the south. I am not cold-I am frightened.

"More than that, two women are dead, and the killer, dead also. We won't know what really happened until Maria gains her full recollection, and, of course, the killer, Rebekka, will never talk.

"I suspect the cop might know more than he is sharing," James tells me.

"Your mind thinks like that all the time."

"You left without back up Megan, big fail. I'm glad he saved your life when your apparent lack of dueling skills failed you."

"Oh my, lecture. Go ahead. I deserve it. But you know what? I stalled the bitch, like Maria did before I got here. So we all helped."

"I'm sorry. But you need training if you want to fight and fight the bad guys. I seriously mean that."

He put his arms around me and for a good minute I felt safe. I like this. But I also know I need to help some more girls, more girls like Maria. I need training.

CHAPTER SIXTEEN

The investigator questions James. He gives his full answers and concludes that his call made to a friend, which in turn notified the police, saved these missing persons, at least two of the five. He promises to keep his friend out of it, noting that special contacts are just that, special contacts required in time of need. The investigator left that contact off his report after James showed him his papers.

A single bullet to the forehead killed Rebekka. She didn't get to kill victim's no. 3 and no. 4, though, she came close. There she lay with blood pooled around her head with eyes looking up to the ceiling. Mickey didn't even know her that well he tells us. He'd seen her costumes with sequins, she'd even worn them a couple nights before they had sex. He didn't know her family or her past-they hadn't gotten that far. This night and the events came so fast. He pulled the trigger so that this girl wouldn't kill the girl that lay on the ground below. He tells the investigator he had come upon the scene quickly and reacted as same. Just after he pulled the trigger the costume clicked in his mind, and it was then, he realized he'd killed his new girlfriend. Hitting her anywhere else besides the head would not have prevented her from pursuing her intentions. He had been through police training eight months ago and knew this to be the case. The investigator concurred with him but also told him a full review would be required. James and I listen in to all the details.

"I know and I hope I did the right thing. I believe I did."

Still he had to go and look Rebekka over and assist the other policemen.

"What a bloody scene straight out of a horror movie." I said.

"I do miss my little Hope."

"How did you get hooked up with this woman?" asks the investigator.

"That's a long story but my brother Joe was there. He might remember it better than me."

"Why is that?"

"Because that's when I hit rock bottom. I blacked out and woke up in a hospital five days later."

"And they let you become a cop?"

"I didn't tell them."

"Well, you just did."

Mickey lowered his head and went to help with the other victims. *The other two were cold by now and missed the whole show* I thought. I wonder about their loved ones.

Stab wounds to the chests to both women on the left side the investigator points out. The bitch went right for the red chambers, the love aqueducts. I stand back and watch the officers attend to the victims. The swords are swiped for fingerprints, labeled, and placed in bags. Civil war swords Maria had told her. They were heavy and ornate but applicable for usage.

What was I thinking I ask myself? I wasn't. It had been nine years since my dad and I had dueled. Somehow it came back, but how reckless of me and for my kids' sake. I was not thinking.

"I forgot about my kids." I pull out my phone and begin to call home.

"I had Nate take care of that. He sent his sister over to sit on the couch until we all come back." James stands next to me, knowing we should leave the scene pretty soon.

"I'm sending Maria via ambulance to the hospital; she's probably okay but should be observed for shock. You can likely pick her up tomorrow, Megan, if everything goes well," said the investigator.

"Thanks. Will do."

"We found the liquid Xanax-she apparently gave it to all the victims, tied them up while they were drowsy and later tortured them, I suspect."

"Why?"

"That is always the question. But we can't ask her-so that will be a mystery. Maria holds some of that and tomorrow she will remember much more. It takes a day or two and then everything floods the mind."

"What a disaster!" I say out loud. And inside I felt a release of pleasure to be still alive. I didn't need to get involved like this-I had my kids to think about. I must stay in the background and not out front.

James leaves the next morning for a business trip He tells me he will be gone for a week. I decide to still go on my girl's trip to Biloxi to play some blackjack and give my talk. Maybe getting away will clear my mind I think. My mother sent me some money to go to this resort and the $225.00 from the talk would be my spending money. The kids are to be with my ex-so all is good. But first I have to check on Maria at the hospital. Mickey gets fired for not revealing his blackout and hospitalization, and gets further examined by investigators for more untold truths. While his brother Joe is questioned about his whereabouts the night before and what does he know about his brother? The investigators go to the hospital but are unable to further question Maria. They tell them to come back in another day or two. I call Maria's mother to come and bring Hope to sit with her daughter. The investigators tell me they think possibly Rebekka was a "wanna" be heroine-that she was seeking recognition from her new boyfriend or others. She apparently stole the liquid Xanax from a previous boyfriend and held onto it for a later use.

The investigator gave Maria's phone back to her which was really the one James left at my house, and she gave it to her mother. Maria's mother gave the phone to me saying she wouldn't be needing it for a while. "Gracias, Megan."

"I'm going away for a few days, so you can stay at my house while she's in the hospital. My boys are with their grandma and grandpa."

"Bien, bien."

Maria is heavily sedated when I visit and the nurses say she will be for a couple more days. They were hoping she could avoid a psychosis. I didn't know how to take that but it sounded serious. I decide to go on my trip and come back later to visit, in that she probably would need me for the long term, and wouldn't even know I was there while heavily sedated. The doctors assure me as such.

Leaving town with my friend felt like an escape. I soon forgot the nightmare that had enveloped my life like an overdue bill which threatened to turn off the services so desperately needed for a comfortable life. Only people are now dead and I have nothing to compare that with except how my father lived every day of his life. I reflect and think he was braver than any of us knew. My eyes are now open.

CHAPTER SEVENTEEN

Biloxi never looked so good. It had the beach, the weather, the surf, the shore, a pool, and gambling with booze. Not that I partook too much but the thought of adult vices was a relief. I enjoy the gambling but really just the adult atmosphere was what turned me on. Lights, people, games, money, music, and the thrill of winning. I hate to lose-so I only play with a certain amount. Truly I am a lightweight when it comes to gambling. As soon as I hit the downstairs after unpacking, following the road trip in my friends light green Cadillac, I order a raspberry lemonade martini. This was the suggestion of the waiter. I sip it and look out upon the wrought iron fenced garden. Yes, I have died and gone to heaven. Wait a minute! I thought seriously about that first date all over again and out at the marble place where I just about died! Did I really want to get into this kind of business?

"Oh no."

"What dear? Are you okay? I know you said you'd be okay, but hell, lady, you almost got yourself killed last week," said Maureen. Maureen was my girlfriend from high school where we met at church in the basement. Her husband was an agent working for the government in some capacity but she wouldn't divulge which unit. She thoroughly grilled me on the "Are you sure you want to get into the dangerous business of law enforcement?"

"Yes. Yes, I'll be fine. I'm forgetting about it for now. I do wonder if that kind of business is for me."

"Truly, you are not thinking of being a cop?"

"Not a cop but maybe investigations or undercover spying. What do you think? Would I be good?"

"Probably, but it could be dangerous."

"The world is dangerous for sure."

"How about that new boyfriend? Maybe he's the one." Maureen kept questioning me always getting me to talk- even if I didn't feel like it. Maybe I should tell her to knock it off. After all I was in a delicate state with what happened to my roommate and myself. I was lucky to be alive.

"Yeah, he might be. But I still need to find a job for me, something I'm good at, something I excel at."

"Cheers lady!" Maureen clinks glasses with me.

"I do excel at Black Jack. Let's go."

"Not before we order another drink from our waiter-he made the best martini this side of Texas."

We order another and head for the casino in the back. Along the way we purchase tickets for a special show in the theatre room on our last day here. I was having fun just walking, talking, and leaving motherhood behind again for a few days. I hadn't had a break in seven years, so it was time for me. One does not know the complexities of being a mom and how engaging it is until one gets away. Surely, I'm not the only one to think this. But no one really tells you what all is entailed. It's like babysitting 24/7 and no one ever does that. They take the money and go home, forget about the children. But when you are a mom it's always lit. Thank goodness I loved them to death. I guess you could say I bonded right away with all my children.

I considered myself a real mom, a mom who went into the trenches and came back out again. I told myself I was cut to be a mom. The role fit perfectly. I was told by others to do something for me or I would lose me. *No losing me now* I thought. Vegas has nothing on Biloxi. What happens here stays here? I laugh and continue walking with my friend.

We spend hours letting go of our money in small amounts and then I stumble upon the card games. I have to watch for a while and learn it because Black Jack I know but poker no way. The table was a mini version of poker-so I study and study. The attendant pushes me saying, "Come on, you're ready. I'll help you."

I sit down and play a hundred dollars. Whatever I win goes in one pile and the losses are just that. Losses. The drink lady comes around a few times and I got my comfort level going while the table fills up with men of all types. At least the game goes slower with more players. That way I wasn't going to lose my money so fast and have to get up and leave. When I tip my waitress for the third and last drink I thought about James and wonder how his evening is going? I should call him later or maybe he'll call me. I guess I would just wait this out. I started to think that I hadn't partied this much since college.

Across the tables and attendants area was another table just like ours. There sat a suitable guy in exactly the same seat as myself. Very cute and playing all by himself. He must know what he was doing as I would never play by myself. I leave the table after I cut my losses, tip the attendant, retrieve fifty dollars, and set out to find my friend. I just happen to walk past the really cute guy. He was still at the table all by himself, poor thing. But I don't play with an empty table and I wasn't looking for a date.

I could not find my friend and decide to take a break

from the smoky room and go out near the swimming pool I'd seen on the elevator billboard. I exit the elevator but not before I saw a lady with long dark hair wearing a bulky multi colored sweater waiting to come aboard. I'd seen her before but where? Don't think about it, it will come to you. And it did as soon as the elevator door shut as I turn around for a second look. How could that be? And was the nice looking young man connected to her? I turn around and head for the pool as I need some fresh air right now. I seem to be the only person headed for the pool and when I get to the doors they won't open. I couldn't go outside. Just then a big man came walking near me. Megan, I think, *what did you do?* Sound the alarm or something? I look in the window boxes located in the hallway for the shoppers trying to compose myself. Things were not normal here-no way, no how. I think this level is off limits, yet it is all lit up. Maybe it's time to go to the room. Maybe my friend went upstairs to our room. Some things were not making sense. Maybe the stress of the last couple events has gotten to me. Where did I see that sweater and on who? Maybe it was from a magazine display. Yes, that was it. It was on different people like swapped out. She must be a plus model with long black hair swept up in a bun atop her head. I saw it on the internet I just know it.

I walk around and head for the elevator to either take me to my room or back down again. I decide upon my room to change clothes. My eyes were red from the smoke filled casino room and my sweater stunk as well. I change and refresh as my friend was still down there. Somewhere. I am getting nervous with the woman in the multi colored sweater, the big man telling me to get off this floor, and the guy sitting all by himself. I feel like I am being watched and I'm on vacation! What is happening? Is this a sting? Did I do something wrong? I feel a little weirded out right now.

I better go find my friend. Then I will feel better. I check the time: 1:45 AM. I better go get her and tell her the time, surely she was tired by now. I know I was and I'd spent $125 that was my tops, no more. My dad sure taught me well in life. Certain things you just have to have a cap on and when it comes to your hard earned money, make sure you spread it out. Have a little fun and stop while you are ahead. Good advice. I'd sure like to win a jackpot. *Maybe I have by not losing* I thought.

I go back down to the big casino room and people were still all over the place. Finally, I spy her over by the penny and nickel machines. Who would play the pennies? My religious friend Maureen, that's who. I was not going to tell her about my slight encounter, these were my issues, and I wasn't sure if I wasn't becoming slightly paranoid since the first explosion with James. Though, he told me to trust my instincts, and tonight they told me I was being followed and watched. They wanted me to play with the young man, a look alike if you will of my ex. I determine he was an actor and I was being lured to play with him. I'm sure the cameras overhead would capture everything. Again, the question is always why? Why because someone doesn't like me and playing dirty was not my cup of tea. But who plays dirty I asked myself? I just didn't know these things but James does. I'll run it by him when I get home. Until then don't alarm your friend-she'll think you are crazy. Am I crazy? Someone wants me paranoid. The dark skinned woman on the elevator was on Maria's site she frequents on the internet. As clear as a bell it was her, no hesitation on my part. Why go after me? They must think I know something about Maria, and her missing brother, or maybe they want a secretive tape on me to frame me? Okay, now your mind is way off. But was it? My head swelled with paranoia. My heart skipped a beat because god damn it this thing was real-yes, I am scared. I am beginning to believe someone wants some dirt on me but I don't have any dirt. I'm pretty clean, maybe not as tidy as a bleached sheet but a good person nonetheless. What if it's the mob? I've heard they are smarter than the law. That's why the law can't get them. I was spinning. Go to bed, this is ruthless and I can't figure it out. Maybe I'll be dead by morning-then I won't have to worry about it. A sweaty layer of moisture covers my hands and core body as this thing played out. I didn't deserve this. I didn't deserve this. Never.

I hate dirty tricks. Probably because I didn't think that way and to think someone wanted to frame me for something I'd never do just infuriated me even more? What on earth? My friend Maureen took me to a burger joint where we met a nice young man straight from Hollywood. He had to write his name down because I forgot it like three times. I guess he gave us more attention than we needed but he was nice. The next day we went walking and toured around other casinos. On the way back my friend became short winded and had to stop several times to catch her breath. I thought perhaps we might have to call 911. Maybe she spent too much time in the smoky casino last night. I want to tell her what happened to me as it was not all in my mind. I saw what I saw what I saw. How devious. How dirty. Maybe I was in trouble. Had I done something wrong that undercover agents were investigating me? What had I done? It had to be police because who would scare you half to death and want to put you in a sting to wait and watch you mess up? Or maybe it was the FBI-they go after lots of folks. This could not be happening to me. I don't take drugs-I'm normal, pay my bills, respect the law, do the right thing, etc. Maybe I had been reading too many novels lately.

I did like those courtroom dramas, politics, and such.

We go shopping for small mementos and I purchase a set of four bar glasses with the fleur de lis symbol etched in them. I love them. They were so pretty. While we shop Maureen got good and bad news in that her sister had had a baby but the child has Down syndrome. This was the most bittersweet moment I think that I had ever encountered in my life. I hug her. We smile, we cry. I was still terrified to think maybe I had done something wrong and wonder again for the hundredth time since 1:45 in the morning who was working against me and for what reason? How can you report suspicious behavior when you think it's the law? You cannot. This made me more terrified. Panic set in and I didn't know what to do about it. But it was real-somebody was following me and they were not stopping.

Maria's mother calls me only once to report that her daughter didn't seem to be doing so well. The nurses were very concerned, doctors, too. They told her to tell me there is nothing I can do at the moment. Possibly she might get better by the time I return. They didn't want to alert me but felt I should know as her roommate and best friend. Also, I did in essence rescue her even though her ex rescued me. Complicated doesn't even begin to describe the situation.

Our last day arrives and we go to the midmorning holiday show. It was spectacular and took my mind off the earlier incidents. I didn't think about it once while viewing but as soon as it was over my mind began to race and my bodies extremities tingled slightly with some sweating. What on earth? I thought to myself I think I am a bit panicked. Scared. I would tell James as soon as he got back from his trip. Maybe I wasn't cracked up to be an investigator as here I was panicked over the possibility that someone was harassing me, and putting me in a choke hold and I didn't know the reason. I need training and reassurance. The sweater was a definite. I'd look over Maria's computer again to find it. Come to think of it-that's probably what they were bugging, especially in lieu of Maria's brother and him being missing. But why me? I thought as the nerve endings throughout my entire inside body became torched with a fiery hot blade I couldn't stop. Breathe Megan. Breathe. The blade is cutting me deeper and I cannot escape. How could my own government be tailing me or causing me distress? Why on earth would they do that? And for what reason. Geez, just come and ask me questions. I will be happy to answer anything for you. I am an honest and nice person, professional, too. It came naturally to me to be good and forthright, I didn't need to try as I always wanted to do the right thing. I now believed that bad people were after me, maybe the law, but bad people that worked in the law. Why would anyone want to perform a sting on me? The nerves in my arms and legs were on fire while they used their whiles to put me under pressure. Gambling is legal last time I checked, so what's the purpose for following me? I am distraught and can think of nothing else. This is not fair. This is ludicrous. America is a great country! Somebody wants something from me that I don't have is the only answer that I can conclude.

Finally, I believe that they want to trick me into doing something I don't normally do. You know when you drive down the road and there's a cop behind you for ten minutes-you drive real careful and start to tense up. Then you are glad when they go on their way. You are relieved and just get on your way with no trouble. Only now, the cop is behind me and doesn't go away. I'm continuously followed and tailed.

The trip home was not as sweet as the trip there. I had had fun right up until the set up. From that moment on I became hyper aware of my surroundings with easements at times and then right back to a heightened state. Was I even in Georgia anymore? This was still the United States except if your own government is after you there's nowhere to go my dear but dig deeper and play along just a little. Don't act frightened or intimidated because that's what they want. Seriously. I told James everything as soon as I saw him.

CHAPTER EIGHTEEN

"Do you believe me?" I ask him. Even I am unsure about it all.

"What does your gut instinct tell you?"

"It's fucking not baby cakes. It's real and that's what scares me! Oh James, what am I going to do?"

James looks at me expressionless, thoughtless. He walks around the room contemplating. This only makes me tingle again with the sword drawn and ready.

I wait for his reply. He stares at me. He gets a glass of water and puts a few ice cubes in it.

He hands it to me in the kitchen and brings my face very close staring into my eyes. He puts the water to my lips and I drink. He whispers in my ear, "I believe you."

I take a big gulp and cough out extra water, gagging just a little. I whisper, "Okay."

I wait and stare. Blankness.

"Go to the concert with your friend tonight. We'll talk after that."

"Tomorrow I want to see Maria. Okay?"

"We'll both go tomorrow."

The boys went to a sleepover and I found myself going out with another friend to a concert. I suppose you could say this was my lucky week, though, I didn't quite feel like it. It did feel good to get out. Certainly, I deserve this break. Yes, I did, I told myself. Quit feeling guilty for trying to have some fun. Motherhood can do that to you my friend told me. Anna and I were going to see a very popular chic, swing across the fans above, and sing her rocking little heart out. I won the tickets at the grocery store where they had a raffle. How sweet.

"You won?" Screamed the boys two weeks ago.

We walk for an eternity to get to our seats. "Pink is going to be awesome. I hear she gets on a trapeze and swings through the air. I can't wait!"

"Not much more time to wait. How great you won these tickets!"

"My boys made me sign up. They saw the table at the grocery store advertising some new gadget, so I did. Then I won."

Anna and I stand up singing and swinging to the tunes we like the best, realizing she had so many of them gave us a great workout. Amazing that she could dangle from a rope and glide through the air over top of all of the concert goers seated below. We had a box seat and the view was the best. We were up in the air with her so it seems.

"I'm sure PINK is exhausted," I said. "I loved it. Thanks for coming girlfriend."

"I wouldn't miss it. You're welcome!" We took pictures with our cell phones to remember this night.

James texts me ... Hope you're having a great time; can't wait to see you later.

Me ... I can't wait to see you.

James ... What time will I see you?

Me ... About an hour; we are leaving now. Great time.

I send him a picture of the two of us.

I drop Anna off and wave goodbye. Anticipation

mounted with each turn as I sped home. I couldn't wait to see James and give him some love tonight. The concert excited me and the thought of him drove me crazy. I hope to see him naked very soon.

This dating thing was good and tonight nothing else existed except me and him. No kids, No Maria. No Hope. No phones that track your every move nor would be-wanna be heroines dressed to the nines with exotic sequined outfits, and long flowing red hair, not to mention drop dead bodies in bodices none of us could wear wanting to kill you.

Well, I could wear them but not many others. My mind went to the bitch that almost killed me. *Megan, you could have been killed.* I knew now that I needed training and tomorrow I would ask James about that.

I turn on my favorite station and drive the rest of the way home with lights flickering catching my eye reminding me of the specks on the ocean on a bright and sunny day. Reflections of light cast like stars across the ocean, too many to count, all for me giving me strength to defeat any bad guy that ever touches me. I feel as though I'm in a trance. Must be the night, must be the music and where I'm headed.

I stop at the light and wait my turn. Now the seconds pause like minutes and the minutes like hours. I turn up the volume to alleviate my impatience. Miley Cyrus sings a new hit titled, "Malibu." I like this. I listen. Just travel across the bridge and you'll be home.

The song and her voice further alleviate me from my thoughts and recent conditions. I am in a trance like state called love.

James is in the kitchen when I open the door. He winks at me and I walk right over to him and give him my full embrace. He warms me with his arms and body and I melt. I love him. He leads me away and down the hall, then opens the bedroom door. It is full of candlelight and flowers strewn across the bed whose linens are folded neatly down. He has his speaker playing a soft jazz. Our kiss connects us again and the night is ours in my room.

We lay awake listening to the notes of bass played on a saxophone on soft, crisp white sheets after amazing sex.

"Why is sex so amazing?" I ask him.

"Because."

"Because why? Tell me."

"Megan, it just is sweetheart."

"No it's not."

"Then you tell me what makes it amazing."

"You."

James laughs a low moan and turns to me, "You get me going girl. There's no stopping. You got me here all night, honey."

"Good, I'm ready for an all-nighter." James turns me over and we roll almost to the edge as my desire increases more and more.

The concert must have put a spell on me as I am totally here for James. He anticipated my return and we join together, over and over. We are both in love I can tell. How did this happen? I dreamily close my eyes and surrender. The room has no walls or doors only soft billowy clouds of ecstasy that ripple through my body as he touches me with his hand.

Our lips cannot get enough. We kiss repeatedly whilst our eyes explore the depths of the other's soul. Even our chests have to heave to replace the oxygen running through our bodies. I feel like I ran a mini marathon as our soaked bodies unite in pleasure. Esta bien Megan.

Later I awaken as James speaks in a low tone.

"We forgot to eat," he mumbles.

"What?"

"I made you an omelet earlier; I thought you might need to eat."

"I'll go warm it up for us," I say. "Be right back."

Just then while I'm in the kitchen the phone rings. I look at the microwave and its 2:45 in the morning. I look at the number and it's unrecognizable. After I heat up the omelet, I put some strawberries on the plate and pull out the champagne bottle. For some reason I think we should toast a glass of bubbly. Then I see my cell phone is ringing.

It's my mother! What? At this hour I question. I answer quietly thinking she might be having some trouble. She answers and says, "Did you just call me Megan? My phone rang and it was your number. I didn't make it in time."

"No mom, I didn't call you but it is nice to hear your voice. I hope you are okay."

"I'm fine. Nice talking to you, too. Come visit me with those kids sometime. You know I can't leave grandma here alone as she can't travel."

"I know I will. Goodnight, love you."

"Goodnight," says my mom.

I miss her. I should go see her but it always seems like trouble and then she has a fit and wants us to leave. So why bother? I shake my head. It's the way it is and always will be. Better to visit by phone at three o'clock in the morning. I walk into the bedroom and find a naked man greeting me with open arms. This I like. My heart is on fire and there's no putting it out. Thank you James.

We toast our glass of champagne, eat our eggs and fruit, serving each other while our skin occasionally touches and sets off small shocks of electric vibes. *Karma is good tonight* I think.

Eventually we fall asleep, pulling the sheets with an

encased light blanket over our love spent bodies, and easing into each other's skin fully reclined. Dreams escape us because we have made our dreams come true tonight.

CHAPTER NINETEEN

Maria's phone rings on top my dresser which wakes both of us. I forgot I set it there when her mother returned it to me.

I go to retrieve it thinking it might be her mother calling me but it was an anonymous caller. The ID said anonymous. *How strange* I thought. I placed it back on the dresser.

"Good morning."

"Good morning," he says. He kisses me lightly on my cheeks just below my eye. I smile.

"I wish this could last 24 hours," I say.

"Me too. It could you know. Someday."

We smile at each other and realize the day is at hand.

James rises and goes to the phone on my dresser. He picks it up. "Megan, this is the phone I left here last week."

"Yes, it is. The number was displayed, so I let Maria use it and then her mother returned it to me at the hospital. I was going to ask you. I'm sorry I forgot."

"You mean she had it the night of the triple murder at the marble house by the river?"

"Yes, I hope you don't mind. Is it okay?"

"Sure. No problem. I do need to return it though; I'll take it from here."

"Okay. Let me see what time we can go visit Maria."

"Perfect. I'll shower real quickly."

"We can eat lunch after we visit her. Let's just be on our way and get a coffee to go."

I quickly shower following James and pull my hair back, wet and all. We take James's car and head for the hospital. He parks the car and we walk swiftly to her room, push the door aside saying her name softly as we enter. Except there was no Maria. The room was empty. Void. We look at each other with questioning expressions. Then we walk straight for the nurse's desk.

"We'd like to ask about our dear friend and roommate Maria 'Alana' Antigua. Where is she?" I say.

"I believe our number is on the list to be called about any news. We are the caretakers of her daughter, along with her mother," James says.

"Yes. Let me get the facilities name and number where she has been transferred."

"Transferred?"

"Yes, her mother went with her. I'm sure they will be calling you very soon. It just happened," said the nurse.

"Is she okay?" I ask.

The nurse, for the first time, looks at me and shakes her head from side to side. "No, she is not okay. She likely will be in the future, I'm fairly certain, but for now she is not."

"What happened?" James persists.

"I can't tell you everything but it is not good at the moment. Would you like me to get the doctor on the phone?"

"Actually, just tell me in your own words, so I can go be with her as soon as possible."

"She had a very dark spell. We have been worried about a psychosis occurring from the trauma that she experienced."

"Yes, go on."

"I'm afraid it happened at four am this morning. She has been transferred to a psychiatric facility and is heavily sedated."

I search this nurses eyes for any sign. How could this happen? But of course this could happen. She experienced a dreadful night over a week ago.

"Here is the site where she will be."

"Thank you," I whisper.

I look at James and cannot believe what is happening. Maria, of all people does not need any more bad luck in her life. We leave the hospital feeling desperate without much hope.

James speeds across town and heads into the big city of Atlanta. I have never been to this facility, and we have no idea where it is. But we keep driving, looking out the window, secretly hoping that this isn't real. This is a bad dream.

I turn off the blaring music in the car while my thoughts race forward to what I might see. Will she recognize me? I should check the internet for psychosis. I do.

"Stress and trauma contribute to a psychosis, it says," I tell James.

"Absolutely, and if it is that then it can be cured."

"Thank you for your calm reassurance." I retort.

"You're welcome."

I reach over and touch his hand and hold it for a moment. "I'm looking forward to the lake house next month, just you and I."

"The lake house will be very nice, Megan. No drama or episodes of violence, rest assured."

We land on Peachtree Street and race even faster, making a few lights, then turn twice and head down an alley. I have never been here before. The street is quiet with no cars.

James pulls up and we see a small sign The Howard Hotel.

"I suppose the name is there to not give away the actual nature of the business."

"I don't know. Seems strange to me," says James. "But this is it, let's go."

We pull in the drive and make our way around back-the place is entrenched in trees and bushes. It's quiet and rather serene. I think about Maria. Don't get more attached Megan. Visit. Make contact. Let the professionals do their business. I say a quick prayer she will be okay. Then I think about Hope. Where is Hope I wonder?

We exit the car and walk the cute little path right up to the back door. We knock as we look around while standing on the back brick patio with chaise lounge chairs, patio furniture with cushions, and flower pots along the edges. The impatience are medium but I'm sure will swell in size by August's end. I feel a bit surreal at this moment. When I look at James he gets the same feeling.

"Bizarre is all I can think at the moment," he says to me.

"I agree."

CHAPTER TWENTY

A woman answers the door and looks us over. "May I help you?"

"Yes, you can. Have you been delivered a patient named Maria Alana Antigua?"

"You know her?"

"Yes, we are on her to call list from the hospital."

"Sure, please come in." She directs us in to a small waiting area with chairs and desk. She sits down and pulls out a ledger and asks for our ID's. We gladly hand them over and she makes copies, then gives them back.

"Let me welcome you to our homelike acute setting. We have Maria and several others. This is a six room facility with five patients and a couple of nurses who live here also."

"Really? They live here?"

"You see these patients have been determined to not be harmful, are experiencing most likely an acute psychosis which should correct itself with a peaceful, homelike environment."

"Is there a doctor on the premise, as well?"

"No but he is a short distance away and we have nurses' aides and orderlies scheduled around the clock."

"You are so calm. When can we see her?"

"Very soon, though, she may not recognize you for a

week or so. Please don't be shocked. Just speak with her and keep the conversation short and not confrontational."

"Okay, but what if I start crying. Will that be okay?"

"Yes, just turn away so it doesn't upset her. She's heavily sedated right now so you probably won't have a conversation that concludes to anything."

"We can do that Megan. We will keep it light."

"These conditions mostly work out very well. The brain is confused by trauma, stress, hormones, etc. It just needs a couple weeks of tranquility and she will be back to normal."

"Wow. Can you be my nurse when I get ill?"

She smiles. I feel like Maria is in good hands. Let's go. I'm ready. I take a deep breath and stand up.

"Please follow me. You can stay fifteen minutes for the first visit."

She takes us up a staircase out near the front of the hotel, rather hospital. It's a grand staircase like in an old house. I realize this is an old house all fixed up. Very nice. Stay calm I tell myself. We climb the stairs. Then at the top we walk along the banister and head for the room furthest away. The nurse unlocks the room from the outside. My breath catches my lungs and I make a sound, a light gasp. It's just that she's locked inside like a prisoner, or maybe a child who has been punished for an hour. I don't know what to make of this. Safety Megan. Safety.

It's then as we walk towards her door that I hear the music. It's opera playing overhead. My dad liked opera I recall. It's lovely. I think if I woke up after a drugged out sleep I might like to hear opera, fluffy pillows, and opera, with smiling nurse faces.

The room is perfect. We walk through the doorway and see Maria asleep in the large overstuffed bed. It has pillows galore, beautiful bedding, four posters and a large window with seating right underneath. I see stuffed animals, dolls, and story books ... like for children. Every color is soft and palatable. The lighting is muted too. Just enough light. The nurse takes us over to Maria and we look upon her. She sleeps very peaceful. I do see an IV in her arm and take notice.

"That was from the hospital and will be removed when she wakes. We expect she will eat and drink just fine."

"If everything is so fine, then why is she here?" I have to ask. I want to know. "Why can't she just come home to us and sleep in her own bed?"

"It does look that way doesn't it? She is monitored, the room is monitored, and needs that for about a week. Then she'll understand what is going on and with some talk therapy we'll get back to her original self."

"Like I said, if ever I get sick come take care of me. Please!"

Maria turned a little and opened her eyes. She looked towards us and then closed them again.

"That may be it for twenty four hours."

"Then how often can we come and see her?"

"You may come every day, once a day, as you like. Once she awakens and sits up you may stay longer."

"Thank you. May I kiss her forehead or cheek?"

"Very quietly or lightly. Yes."

This pleases me. I hand my purse to James and walk over to my roommate, my friend. It seems there is hope and I am grateful. I lean down to kiss her on the head above her left ear. Her hair is pulled back and I see that she has a sore on her ear. I'm startled but kiss her lightly on the head and retract myself.

I get James attention and point to the ear so he notices. He looks perplexed.

We graciously leave Maria in the best of hands. We all head back down stairs and I notice the nurse locking her door again. She sees me and says, "After the medication wears down and she becomes aware of where she is it won't be locked."

We thank the nurse and give her our number to call for anything she needs. We go to leave.

"I almost forgot. Where's her mother and Hope?"

"They were here and have gone home as they were with her at four am when her psychosis hit. The hospital had to medicate her with Thorazine, Haldol, and a light sedative. They decided to go rest and come back tomorrow."

"Good idea."

"Yes, we suggested that. However if they felt the need to they could come back anytime to look upon her."

We say goodbye and walk to our car.

"Very bizarre," says James.

"Spot on," I agree.

CHAPTER TWENTY ONE

We are silent for most of the way back to my place. Until I bring up what I saw. I suddenly feel guilty. I begin to cry, loud sobbing cries.

"Hey, what's the matter?"

I sob some more and try to wipe my tears away. I can't I feel so bad. "Oh James. I didn't believe her about her phone. Did you see the red sore on her ear?

"I did."

"That has to be from her phone. What else?"

"I suppose but she threw it away last week."

"The camera must have turned on and caused her to have a burn area. Is it possible?"

"I have no idea. But my inside man will know. I'll ask him?"

"I didn't believe her. She did use your phone though for a week. Would someone have turned that phone on? Where did you get that phone anyway?"

James stares at me in thought.

"She used it the whole week from the time she threw hers in the water until the tragedy at the marble house by the river."

James looks at me very curiously and deep in thought.

"Sweetie, I need to visit my guy like right now."

"I just remembered something."

"What? What is it?"

"She had to keep plugging the phone in to recharge it as it lost juice rather quickly."

"I'm listening."

"I didn't think anything of it-just that it must be a derelict phone you found."

"That doesn't begin to describe this apparent nightmare we seem to be experiencing."

"Can you go on another date with me to our first place we met?"

"Are you sure? When do you want to do this?"

"I was hoping we could go there tonight."

James picks me up and tells me no phones or devices. "This is a plain old date Megan."

"All righty then. Same place different outcome." I laugh for no apparent reason other than to suppress my fear.

"Altered outcome. We come home, no explosives. Promise."

"Promise?"

"To the best of my ability."

This time we sit up at the bar and it's filled with people. We talk a little about Maria, Hope and her mother. They have visited and she is starting to wake up. I plan to see Maria tomorrow.

James is staring at me. Quite a lot.

"Is everything okay?" I ask.

"No. It's not." He pauses.

I stare back at him and see that he is extremely troubled.

"I have to ask you something. Okay?"

"Sure. Go ahead." I have no idea and wonder if I should be scared or something. I think to myself. I hope he is who he says he is. One last moment of tension before he spills the beans, I think.

"Some friends of mine are going to come in here and talk with us in a few minutes. These are the people I met up with last week while you were gone. We are going to act like we are old friends. They and myself. You are just meeting them for the first time. It will be fine."

"Okay. And what?"

"You know you said you were looking to get into a new business."

"Yes?"

"They are my buddies from the old days, my previous life from the special forces."

"And why do they need to meet me?"

"With your go ahead they want to formulate a plan to spy on someone."

"Spy. Hmmm."

"You are already targeted, I'm sorry to say. Because of Maria's brother they have come near you, and now, the phone you borrowed has picked up your voice and activities. Possibly, they think you know something about Maria's brother. He took something from them a while back and they want it back. It must be valuable because they keep trying. Some even went to prison for a while, now they are out. That's it."

"That's it?"

He didn't know what to say.

"I'm not ready."

"You're right. You're not."

"Why don't you think I am?"

"Cause you said you're not."

"Am I ready? To get the bad guys?"

"As ready as you'll ever be. If you think about it, you won't do it."

"Who is going to protect me?"

"I will. I'll be there right by your side. At all times."

"At all times."

"James, great to see you."

"You as well."

"This must be Megan, right?"

"Yes, please join us."

Suddenly, I'm sitting right across from two young guys about my age and engaging in little conversations. One is drawing a map on a napkin talking about his days hunting in the woods and the other begins talking about sword fighting.

"I heard you fight with swords."

"I have a long time ago, then again, more recent. Just about got myself killed."

"I heard about that. You just hadn't practiced in a long time. I think we should practice tomorrow. What do you think?"

"Yes. I guess I would like that."

"James is going to have to go visit another friend for the day. He can join us after we duel."

"Ever handled a gun?" The other one asks me.

"No, don't like guns."

"That's okay. How about knives?"

"Yes, I can handle knives. I practiced throwing them at fairs, all over Georgia, for fun you know."

"Like throw them and miss the people kind of fun?"

We all laugh. The tension is broke. Thank God. What am I getting myself into?

On the way home we stop by his little out of the way hidden shop to visit his friend Nate.

Unbelievably, he's there at nine thirty at night. "Megan, you can come in. You should meet him. He knows everything and he's about your age."

I get out of the car and step through a threshold into the night. Once inside I realize my life was changing forever. Nate steps out and greets us like we were guests at his store, which we were. But not any guests, special guests. Special Forces. I was the extra baggage, the carry on, the guarded lore of noir. Am I going to get in the way? I hope not.

"Greetings, my man," says Nate. Nate is an eye glass speckled young man, very disheveled on the outside. But when he spoke, he spoke like a nuclear scientist making a bomb so small it might be the size of a feather. But he wasn't into bombs, he was into helping his friend make conquests, conquests of the spying nature. Like James Bond has his secrets, Nate invents those for James. "Hello, you must be Megan."

"Hello Nate, nice to meet you. You going to let me in on the goods, the plan?" I smile. I tease. But James looks at me dead serious for a moment. Then he breaks out laughing and hugs me with his spare arm.

"You are going to know what you need to know. You are on a need to know basis. If you pass this first assignment, you're in. Then you'll know some of what I know," James explains.

Nate gives him a small device and tells him to wear it on his shirt tag from the neck area and for me to talk into it when I need to correspond back. Nice. I am involved. I can do that. But hey when are we going to get into trouble?

He also gives him a woman's compact-filled with spy devices he explains.

"Thanks. Not sure where I'll be using these but awesome."

"Here, you two will need these." Nate hands us new phones. He assures us they are only bugged by himself with a direct line to his boss.

"I didn't think you had a boss Nate."

"I am my own boss, but when it comes to my man here, the one and only James the Bear, well, I have to have a little help. You know he gets himself caught in all kinds of places."

I wink at Nate and he winks back. We leave with our new supplies and head home.

"Tomorrow I will be back before dark or just after. Good luck dueling."

CHAPTER TWENTY TWO

The next morning James leaves early to make a flight for an unknown destination. He could not tell me and I did not press him further. I was content. I was going to learn my first real operations as in the spying kind. There was much for me to know, that I knew. *Maybe I should read a book on spying* I thought. I prepare a large breakfast as everyone would be here this morning: my kids, Maria's mother, and Hope. I made bacon, and eggs, French toast, fruit salad, and fried green tomatoes. I even prepared a Hollandaise sauce for us adults to put over the eggs atop the fried green tomatoes with crab cakes. This, I declared, the biggest meal I'd made since I met James. Maybe I should cook for him sometime. Nah, not at first. He might get used to that. I'd save that for later.

"What you smile about Miss Megan, this morn?" asked Maria's mother Gladys.

"Oh, you caught me thinking about James, my new boyfriend."

"That a good thing he make you smile? You is happy!" She laughs. Me too.

My boys were home now from camp and we had a week to ourselves. Then we would all go to the lake house James has rented. The boys would stay for the Fourth of July then go to their grandparents place for three weeks. I would miss them terribly but a break is a break and it didn't cost a thing, while the boys got to know grandma and grandpa. My ex would get to spend good summertime fun with them, too. Win. Win. Win. I had to admit, despite the initial turmoil and Maria's condition, I hadn't had this much help since before the kids were born. I was taking it all in. I deserved every last moment.

I google spying and undercover operations trying to see what I might be getting myself into. Surveillance shows up and I read about it. There was all sorts of equipment and I read about some of it. I'm sure top secret things are not for sale on the internet. That's what I surmise anyhow.

I'd been to see Maria twice and would stop by today for a quick visit. Then I'd go see her before we left for the Fourth of July. Her mom and Hope would stay at my place while I was gone. She was still in a daze and not really looking at us. The nurse reassured us again it would take about five more days to become clearer, in all about two weeks. We all waited. She looks good. She is eating, not talking, but walking around her room. The doctor sees her every day and nurses take good care of her. Later this week would be about 12 days or so. Maybe then I'd see a glimpse of Maria.

I shower and prep for my duel today with James's friends. Maria's mother would watch the kids and give them a snack. I tell them I'll be home to make dinner. She could go visit Maria for dinner and maybe eat with her.

His friends pick me up and we head for a private club they work out in. The sports car sped away and squeals just a bit. Impressive. Yes. We pull into a private residence and walk in. Maybe this was their place, not sure. They gave out no answers. They show me to a room where I could pick out some equipment for protection. So I did. Before putting it on we head for a weight room and they want to see what kind of weights I could hold up.

I was fairly strong as I worked out a lot during my latter high school years and college. Even during my pregnancies I managed to hit the gym and stay strong. One of them stood over by a boxing punch bag and punched away. I lift what I could with ease and then the other guy added some more weights.

"Let's see what Megan can do?"

"Go for it!"

"Sure, watch me."

After a warm up and a little bit of punching we put our safety gear on and he hands me a sword. "We'll just take it slow."

I nod. And then we prance around dueling with each other in a light fashion. He was strong. He goes slowly and I adjust as it had been many years. I was rusty but I had memory. And he commented during a break as such.

James interlude ...

James passes the outside clearance and then through the double doors on the inside. He was in. He met his boss after the secretary announced his presence.

"James, how nice to see you."

"Likewise."

"How is your leave of absence going? What were you taking three to six months after 13 years' service? You deserve it. You were doing great things on highly selective projects most of your time here at the Special Forces."

"Yes. Six months leave."

"What can I do for you today?"

"I came because I have a lead or tip on an old case that I thought we wrapped up a few years ago."

"Go on."

"It's not real active but I think maybe there is a bad cop or FBI badgering a young woman. I'm uncertain, but I don't know who else would want to harm her because of her roommate's brother."

"Listening."

"You may have heard about our triple murder by the river done by a diva wanna be. She was actually dating the cop who killed her point blank. He saved my girlfriend."

"What on earth? Yes, I heard about the triple murder done by a loony zany broad. He saved your girlfriend?"

"The girl I'm dating, Megan, was sparing with her using civil war swords at the marble place by the river up in Tate, Georgia. Incredible actually. The zany broad had already killed two ladies that dated her cop boyfriend. She was out for blood."

"Let me finish. Your girlfriend tried to save the day and didn't. Cop comes, sees she's about to go down and he saves the day. Were you there?"

"Of course."

"The villain is dead, your girlfriend is alive," his boss says.

"And I clean up the mess. Yup. But there's more. The hero cop has a brother who has it out for the missing brother of my girlfriend's roommate."

"Run that by me one more time," his boss asks.

"My girlfriend's roommate has a brother who stole something, likely cash, from this cop and others. He's wanted to find him for a long time. The zany broad got wind of this and decided to try and take down the roommate, clearing the way for her, and then no one could find the brother. Then she'd have the cops undivided attention, and love, I guess."

"You think maybe there's a ring of nonsense out there

still hanging on to finding this dude."

"Maybe you could help us get them from bothering normal folks."

"You've come to the right place. But you know that."

"How's that?'

"The surveillance has been kicked up tenfold since you left two months ago. It's in full gear, and I mean it's like we own the states and beyond."

"Seriously?"

"Yup. Right now. Here today. 911 is never going to occur again, ever. Never."

"That part is good. But who is watching the viewers, the spies?"

"Trust, we have to trust our own. But that is a good question for future reference. See ... we need you. Come back and I'll set you on that task force."

"I'll think about that. For now I'm going to give you the plan set out by myself and two buddies, Roger, and Edgar, along with my secret coder I always use. You should be able to take them down over a two week period if they take the bite. And I'm sure they will." I instruct my boss.

"Got it. Let me show you around. I'll hand this off to a special agent you can trust."

As we make our way around the facility, I take note of the advancements made over the last couple months since I'd left. Lots of surveillance, lots of new people, and lots of monitors.

"Hey, hold up, let me take this call."

We stop and wait for his call. I check my cell for the time.

"The agent just read the project and wants you to meet someone, if you have time. I know you have a flight home later today."

"Sure."

"Yes, I'll send him the name and place. Send it to me."

CHAPTER TWENTY THREE

"Hello Nate. What's up?"

"I know you are on your way home. I was the one interfacing with you and your boss. I found a special lady interested in you and she wants to talk with you in private."

"When?"

"Like right now on your way home from the airport."

"Okay, am I close?"

"I'll text it into your phone and then you hit the link. You're welcome."

"Thank you. Be in touch."

"Megan. Hello."

"Hello James."

"I'm on my way back but I'm going to be a few hours late. I have a client to meet and then I'll come right to see you."

Silence.

"I can't wait to hear about the sparring with the swords today."

"And I cannot wait to tell you!"

"See you then."

"Later."

James found himself once again in Buckhead in the same week. He knew the area as a youth with a driver's license.

Yes. He used to cruise Buckhead searching for chicks on the weekends right after his senior year before he joined the police force, then later volunteered for the navy and became a member of the Special Forces. Seems like a long time ago but actually it was only sixteen years ago when he set out make his dreams come true. Sometimes he thought he was so busy he forgot to make time for himself. So here he was on a six month sabbatical. Because of his stature and accomplishments they didn't want to lose him but saw that he needed a few months to sort things out. He'd lost both parents when he was overseas out on the high seas, if you will. That was his family, no one else existed. His boss tried to be his father at times, thus he said take this time I have it approved from the highest authority. Find yourself were his exact words. James didn't know he needed finding, but he was enjoying his friendship with Megan and his extra time off. He was ready to call her his girlfriend, then again that might mean commitment. So be it.

He knocked on the door and he could hear the chimes ringing loudly throughout the first floor. This was a mansion with hedges and a circular drive centered by a large fountain spraying water on this afternoon in late June. He had no idea what this was all about but he was told to meet this woman that could maybe help him with Maria. That seemed far-fetched. But this month was on the crazier side of normalcy.

A gentleman answered the door.

"Please come in. We've been expecting you for a short while."

"Thank you."

"I'm Jesse, may I take your jacket?"

"Nice to meet you, I'm James. I'm good."

"As you wish. Let me tell her you're here."

The butler retreated and before long he returned.

"Please follow me. She's in her office." The gentle butler named Jesse wore a white summer suit with similar colored shirt under topped with a bowtie. Quite mannerly, he had graying hair and wore eye glasses halfway down his nose. I believe the disposition with which he routed himself through the mansion gave him proper exercise in a day. He seems to have a jolly expression in the gaze of his eyes. Yes, his eyes were quite happy as though he enjoyed this day to day exertion known as his job.

James follows Jesse up the long circular stair case. What is it about these old homes and the grand staircases? He looked around and everything was neutral muted with greens and greys. Very nicely done with draperies and exquisite paintings. He saw the dining room was dark navy with paintings of boats, and such, like a dark sea with brass items. Once upstairs the tone changed slightly to be more dramatic with color. The butler stopped and knocked at a door, and, James paused, stood, and waited. He heard footsteps from inside the wooden floor walking to the door.

The butler addressed the lady, and nodded, then swept his gloved hand over to me. How formal. James was not expecting this. Not today. Not after flying. He smoothed his hair and hoped he looked appropriate. Maybe he should have googled her. In his rush of sorts he forgot to do his homework. "James, you're slipping." He whispered to himself. Then walked through the entryway into a brightly lit room, a red room.

"Please come in. I'm thoroughly glad you made it, found it that is." A most pleasant voice greeted him. He stirred inside and he felt that his voice might be shaky. This woman was dressed to impress. She had a beautiful gown on that you might wear to a most special event. She walked toward him.

James pulled himself together and briefly wondered what on earth this woman might want with him or why Nate set up this meeting?

Quickly, he scanned the room. Piano. Bed. Sofa. Art. Red color everywhere.

"Hello, I'm James, and possibly, I've made an error. You might have the wrong person." He looked over at the bed and piano.

She saw his eyes. "Oh no."

"Maybe you were expecting someone else."

"Sarah Callais," she saw his eyes flicker. "Yes, *the* Sarah Callais, but you can call me Scarlet."

"Sarah Callais, nice to meet you."

"Likewise," she says.

"James Edward Kelly, ma'am."

"Please call me Scarlet, as I know that we will be friends." He looked at her keenly; she had on a red floral floor length silk gown with high heels and white long sleeve gloves. Her shoulders were covered with a silky champagne colored scarf. Her dark long hair was swept up in a chignon halfway up the back of her head with long tendrils flowing down each side. Her earrings were diamonds-they just had to be and lots of them. A gold band encased her left fourth finger-married? Maybe. And the makeup was especially formal, almost stage like.

"Scarlet, why would Nate want me to meet you? Not that I wouldn't want to meet one of the great opera singers of all times. I'm puzzled."

"We have plenty of time to get everything understood. You can stay two or three hours, correct?"

"Yes, I can. Your butler said we were meeting in your office. Pardon me ma'am, but this appears to be your bedroom."

"This is where I conduct my most serious of businesses, I assure you."

"A place where no one else can hear us, and whatever do you mean serious business?"

CHAPTER TWENTY FOUR

She gives him time to pause as she walks over to the windows and drops the curtains. Meanwhile, he scans the room like he was trained in Germany and other countries. Three large paintings with antique frames, several other nondescript pictures, two candle wall sconces made of brass, beamed ceilings painted red as well, two end tables with multiple stacked books, large books, red on red floral wallpaper with high floorboards for trim, a lighter red short haired rug over a wooden floor with a coffee table centered in the 'business' room. He hadn't even made it to the piano with real candelabras at each end and the bed. He looked over at it again. It was the largest bed he'd ever seen and tall with silk and velvet trimmings, perfectly placed pillows, and adorning the windows red velvet draperies, probably made in Europe or something.

Scarlet turns to him and asks if he'd like a drink. "Yes, whatever you have will be fine I'm sure."

"To be sure I will feed you dinner with an expresso before you leave."

He sees the glass candle sconces on the coffee table and some assorted papers, maybe she had been reading. He walks over to her to obtain the drink then thanks her.

If he didn't know any better he thought the red room

made him feel expressive. He couldn't wait to find out what was on her mind. He took a swift large sip and followed her lead to the sofa, where they sat, and she immediately began talking.

"Someone once gave me the nickname of Scarlet, as I was from the south, I suppose. I use it to my own advantage. No one ever suspects a black Scarlet, but here I am."

"And I suppose with everywhere you have been, and sang, they know how hard you work with a tedious travel schedule. I know you have received awards of every kind."

"How would someone like you know that?"

"I saw them on a hallway wall downstairs behind the staircase."

"I knew I picked the right person, you are very observant. How many pictures with horses on the wall behind you?"

"Two."

"How many pictures of people?"

"Three."

"And how many books stacked on the floor to your right?"

"Eight."

"I like you. Cheers." She sipped her rum drink slowly. James checked out her face. Remarkable and made up, I suppose, for herself and to impress him. She was definitely impressing him. He wondered why she was gaging him with such scrutiny. He was sure she would be telling him very soon.

"Cheers." He wondered if the place was bugged. He looked for clocks, smoke detectors, and wall clocks. None seen.

"I had the place debugged yesterday. I do that on a regular basis."

"You are reading my thoughts. Am I that transparent?"

"I know all about you, everything there is to know."

"Do go on. I'm interested but not in myself."

"Nate intercepted and contacted you yesterday because I wanted to meet you. I think you can help me."

"Tell me what can I do?"

"You all are setting up a sting, Nate told me."

"You want to mix your plans in with mine?"

"Maria's brother is my grandson and I know where he is."

"Now that's a bombshell!" James let out too much expression, but hey, it was a remarkable fact.

"I told you that you are the perfect person to help me."

James swallowed his drink, stood up, walked to the window, and with his hand opened the curtain slightly. He needed a moment to walk it through, thinking about Megan and not wanting her to be harmed in any way. He reflected and began to tell her this.

"If Nate has already sent me here, then I know you are very legitimate. What I have to figure out is if my new girlfriend, yes, girlfriend, will be in harm's way?"

"If you are there she won't be."

"Your confidence is noted."

Scarlet stood and went to the decanter of rum, she retrieved his empty glass and poured him another drink, then handed it to him. "Today you think. You are not working so please enjoy our company together. We both have been all over the world. Allow me a few moments to entertain you."

He nodded in approval.

She went to the piano and began playing melody after melody.

He listened and pondered her words. He relaxed and enjoyed her music. Here he was in a red room with a diva playing beautiful music for him. He smiled. Why not help her? Maybe this is what he was meant to do and to have his new sweetheart by his side. He already wanted to train her but he didn't want to make her tougher than himself. His mind wandered.

He allowed himself to picture Megan and him working together, followed by a long walk on the beach. He even entertained the thought of the two of them fishing out in the Gulf of Mexico. The thought was lovely. He felt calm and smooth at the moment listening to this beautiful woman play the piano for him.

She continued on and on. He thought to himself she sings and plays the piano. Music. He wondered what kind of music Megan liked most of all.

She was coming to a close and looked over at him. He raised his glass and smiled in appreciation.

Scarlet lowered her head and smiled herself. She was enjoying this little flirtatious episode of meeting for the very first time. What a lovely lady. Yes, he would work with her.

She stopped and he applauded. Then stood. She walked over to him and gave him her gloveless hand. "I believe it's time for dinner."

The butler walked in and delivered dinner to them right here in "her office." He set it upon a small table with a white tablecloth. She directed James to the table. He sat after she was seated.

Halfway through a delicious chicken and dumpling meal with green beans almandine she began talking and didn't stop until they were finished and ready for dessert.

"You must be wondering, why me of all people, would want to be a part of a sting-let me tell you everything. Sometimes we give to charities, build schools, and donate to worthy causes. I do all of that. Then a long time ago something happened to me that made a lasting impact. I married a police officer, he was a good one, did things the right way. His partner didn't like black people, even told him so. One night he didn't protect him, didn't cover for him. And my husband died but nobody could prove anything. Someone told me about it later. I forgave his partner not knowing any better. Then it happened again and I told the station, reported what I had heard. It fell on deaf ears. My career took off handsomely; I traveled the world and tried to forget. I couldn't. I had the child my husband would never see, the child would never know his father who was a good man. This child grew up and had a child but never married. That child and Maria have the same father. I do my best for this boy. He had an altercation with the police one night and they put him in jail. I went to see him and bailed him out. The story he told me was absurd. I believed him. There's good cops and there are bad cops. It just is. He told me a bad cop was going to blame him for a crime he didn't commit. I decided to do something about this, with, of course, the law on my side. That's where Nate comes in. The rest is a long story but I help people that are victims. We find the bad guys. It takes time and money and I used to have both. Now I just have money."

"You're dying?"

"That's what they say. Doc gives me a year to live."

"I'm terribly sorry. Very sorry to hear that. Are you sure?"

"If anybody can beat it it's me, that's for sure. I found my calling, and I want to do more, much more."

"I want to help you. Supreme justice and the right side of the law is where I'm at."

"I know."

"This sting is all about that. But I don't have the full plans as yet. Nate will fill me in."

"I'd do anything for this boy. I have him tucked away safely for a while. He's a good kid. My heart yields to these people that don't get treated fairly."

"Maria's mother is your daughter?"

"No, but I do know all about Maria's issue with the psychosis at the moment. That's my mini hospital. I know you've been there."

"Maria's father and your grandson's father are the same. I see. Some distance but connected."

"You've read the papers this month I'm taking," Scarlet said.

"Actually, I haven't. That's part of my six months off. I read a local paper with an explosion headline, that I happened to be in the wrong place at the wrong time."

"I know."

"We escaped. Barely."

"So you don't know the news?"

"I don't what? I've been dating and staying at my girlfriend's house with three boys, and managed to not get killed at the marble place by the river up north."

"James, always get the news. Even if it's one source, know something."

"Okay, I give. What?"

CHAPTER TWENTY FIVE

"I'm assuming Nate and you will have a conversation about this. The story just came out. The biggest scandal to hit Washington and the NSA landed this month. Over two weeks ago a guy named Snowden, a contractor from the NSA, blew the lid off the operations. He's headed to God knows where right now after being in an airport. He gave an interview in some hotel revealing that every citizen was on the table to be spied upon."

"How do you know so much? I haven't heard a thing and I was just there at headquarters in Virginia."

"Because they are keeping a lid on the fire. But it's huge. He's a regular, believable guy, smart too."

"You must have a paper source, a journalist or something?"

"I have my sources, all legit. I operate legit, debugged. You see a TV in here? A clock? A smoke detector? A cell phone? My husband taught me to always be suspicious of everything, except opera. I love opera."

"You're incredible. I mean that."

Scarlet stood and walked over to a tall stand. He'd missed that earlier. She reached for a cd and brought it to him. "This is for you. Listen to it on your way home."

"Thank you. I will."

"People are the same all over the world and no one knows that better than me. Imagine that, a black woman, a diva, as they call singers today who does spying on the side. Nobody would ever imagine that, would they?"

She laughed loud and seemed to be enjoying telling her story.

The butler, Jesse, brought in dessert. Peach and cranberry cobbler with vanilla compote on the side delighted the both of them, followed by expresso as promised.

"Thank you Jesse," she said and added, "I tell him he doesn't have to wear the gloves, act so proper, or be so quiet. He says he likes it this way. My driver on the other hand doesn't stop talking in the car. I think he does that just in case somebody has found me out and is bugging it."

James shakes his head. He laughs and they both rise. This meeting is over. The pair shake hands and James becomes very serious. She stares at his eyes.

"I will be prepared and do the best I can while protecting those that are involved with me."

"I know you will. We will find these bad guys when they come out of the woods, once, and for all." Scarlet relents.

"Thank you for the wonderful meal and piano concerto."

"You're welcome. You'll get the real deal on your way home."

James nods. Jesse, the butler, is at the door to escort him downstairs.

"I see why they nicknamed you Bear," she says.

"The brown eyes and hair?"

"It's the stare, definitely the stare."

With that James was escorted to the front door and handed a business card from Jesse.

Sarah Callais Opera Singer

The Scarlet Sings Her Songs

Agent-Kimberley Callais
#404-800-8000

He started the car, clicked the seat belt, and headed to the most beautiful girl he'd ever met. He headed home to Megan. He was in love. And about to be more in love once he listened to the diva of opera. Smiling he sped away to suburbia.

James stops to get gas on the way back to Megan's place and calls Nate.

"Why didn't you tell me about the NSA?"

"Because you would be troubled by it, bothered for sure, and wouldn't effectively use your capabilities to the fullest. I knew it would be a distraction. The full extent is just being explored and people are scrambling at this moment."

"Go on."

"This next job you're going to do is pivotal. You are going to suspect everyone and in the end-you'll get the bad guys, wherever they are, at least the ones coming out. It's going to give us an idea how widespread this collection thingy is."

"I want Megan's place debugged."

"Got it, though, I don't think it is."

"The cop's girlfriend was going to kill her-somebody doesn't like Maria."

"I've got the plan and only five people will know it. Make that six if you tell Megan."

"The less she knows the better. She's not ready as yet."

"Stop by tomorrow. Ready, set, go for July 5th."

"Perfect, then we'll have the 2nd-4th with the boys."

James get back in the car and thinks about the great time they will have with the boys. Only Nate, himself, Scarlet, and two undercover agents will know the plan. The agents will provide local cops on a need to know basis. He wondered how far up this thing went? He hoped his own boss from headquarters was not involved. Spying for the good of the country against evil was one thing but spying for internal evil, corporations, the mob, other agents, or sexual exploitation was wrong and not good for America. He guessed you just couldn't be certain.

Tomorrow he and Megan would pack up for the three week stay at the lake house he had rented. He also had to go visit Nate. He turned up the volume listening to Sarah, rather Scarlet, sing opera. Enthusiastically the pedal declined more to the floor.

Up 400 North he climbed and maneuvered with ease as there was only slight traffic tonight.

James is relaxed and tells himself he has never felt this free or happy. He says aloud to himself, it must be Megan. He dials her number and says, "I love you."

"James."

"I just wanted to tell you that as soon as I felt it. And I just felt it. I know it's been like only six to eight weeks."

"Seven."

"Thanks for meeting me that first time."

"You're welcome."

"See you in a few minutes."

"Okay."

CHAPTER TWENTY SIX

James arrives before Nate even opens the door to his business. Of course, he brought him breakfast and coffee. James just looks like a typical customer, maybe his older brother or possibly an uncle. The pair walk to the back room and Nate locks the door. Business didn't open until he unlocked the door and he wanted to talk to his main man, his friend, and older brother that he never had.

"Morning Nate, her ya go," says James. Nate closes the door to a tiny little office-a room without windows.

"Thanks big brother and I mean that with brotherly love, the face to face kind, not the spying kind."

"Tell me, when were you going to fill me in on all the 1984 shit happening in Virginia or wherever it's happening?"

"It's not common knowledge, yet."

"You sent me to someone who knows quite a hell of a lot, more than myself."

"She's big. I can't give out that information. She's tied all the way up to the top. She's above me, in fact, she gives me orders, okay?"

"Well, thank you for initiating a meeting. It was good for me. I'd like to do things the right way, and help others, you know get the bad guys, even here in the good old USA."

"Yes sir! You are going to do just that beginning July

5th." Nate is expressive and salutes James.

"Wires are tapped and I'm in? I'm not allowing Megan to know the entire plan. Therefore, she'll just act normal."

"Good thinking. Basically, you all have a good time with the boys, they leave, and Scarlet's boy arrives. He's the lure. His girlfriend is an undercover cop but he doesn't know it. That's for safety purposes."

"And do I know everything?"

Nate looks at James and contemplates this question.

"You know everything you need to know."

"Sure." He trusts his little brother.

James eats his breakfast and drinks some coffee. Nate does the same.

"Nate, I'm really glad your dad introduced us. I got a little brother and you got a big brother."

"This is a great friendship, working or not, we fit. I'm thankful, too."

"What if I move to the coast down in Florida?" James mentions his thoughts.

"You mean like six hours away?" Nate does not seem worried.

"Exactly."

"I'm not going to tell you again. I can go. Anywhere. I want. Anytime."

"But you're still not going to tell me the name of your boss are you?" James persists.

"No, I can't do that and don't try to find out-because it will blow both our covers. I'm serious as shit man."

"Well, I'm sure it's a connection from your dad and I know he was a great guy. Too bad his plane went down." James shakes his head in this sorrow as he meant every word.

"It's okay man. I've told you a thousand times I'm not

stressed by that-leave it alone. It is okay you feel sorry, hell, I feel sorry. But I recovered and my mom still cooks for me."

"You still living at home?"

"Yes, I am. She needs me and I need her to take care of things until I get settled someday. That day hasn't happened yet." Nate smiled at him. His life was actually very good. "Besides, I get nothing but great reviews. I'm a trusted man and that means the world to me."

"Tell me about PRISM." James wanted as much information as he could get, from a great source.

"So you do know about such things. Do I know everything about you that I should know?"

"Nate, you know everything you need to know."

"Okay Bond. We're bonded."

"No kidding. Tell me about PRISM."

"PRISM is the government's back door policy. They gather infotel, information and intelligence, on citizens through Social Medias and cellular modules. It's spying 401."

Nate continues on. "With advanced terrorism around the world, we go and collect conversations from everywhere."

"Sweet."

"But you already knew that. But last year in 2011 something changed, it became different. It became like a wild goose chase, catch it all, use it all, and spy on anyone for different purposes other than government collections."

"In other words, use it for companies, and businesses, not just law enforcement." James concedes.

"Bingo." Nate nails it.

"And. Other people that we either don't like, or their brother is in jail, and maybe the sister is hiding something, or possibly we need to make the family look bad for our case in court." James tries to conjure a worst scenario.

"The government ordered Microsoft, Google, Apple,

Yahoo, Facebook, and You Tube to open its channels for the US government to spy on individuals-even ones they were prosecuting in court, even more so. Does that sound constitutional?" Nate gives him his best reasoning.

"Uncertain. It gives them an advantage to win a case, that's unfair. If someone had a case in the federal courts I don't see how that would be legal et all." James fairness and thought is rising up.

"At the very least its infringement upon someone's privacy. And what if there's a person in law that is acting liking a criminal? They just get away with it." Nate gives James the reason he does his business.

"Smoking gun." James spoke, then the two of them became silent knowing why they worked together so well. It was as if they were the police of the police state.

"Nothing anyone can do about it. That's ruthless. That could kill America and all its idealists. The constitution is supposed to protect us, and the law is supposed to protect us from the bad guys. But if the bad guys are the law then what is a person to do? Go away in chains and suffer, or a certain death by a hit man." Nate carried this heavy burden upon his shoulders, like he knew more than he spoke, hopefully, not too much more as the two of them agreed some of this was not constitutional.

"Scarlet said someone tried to tell their bosses three times of inappropriate actions by agents but nothing was done. So, in essence, they police themselves."

"They have not gotten to the bottom of this release of information. Big Brother is allowed to spy on you at any time with a warrant-not warrantless actions, but they do anyway is what the whistleblower stated."

"Who was it?" asks James.

"Edward Snowden."

"Edward Snowden? Don't know him."

"He's over in an airport or maybe in China or Russia by now. He told his bosses three times and they told him to forget about it. It's the way it is. He couldn't live with himself from what he saw and saw others doing. They were spying on any American at any time: in their houses, their bedrooms, watching them naked, having sex, talking with loved ones. Spying to the thousandth degree by: intercepting phone calls, using video cameras through computers, laptops, on and on. They even went into their houses and planted bugs."

Nate watches his friend take in this news. He knows this affects James because he fought in wars to protect Americans freedoms, in that a government didn't have overreach or abusive powers towards its citizens.

"What about catching the bad guys? Were they watching the bad guys get it on, too?" James is disturbed in ways he cannot even fathom at the moment.

"James, I'm not here to worry about the bad guys over in some other country. My oath is to protect citizens of the United States of America, right here in America. Now, if it's a bad guy with a gun, that's your job. That's your training Mr. Seal."

"What's Snowden's stats?"

"He's a regular smart type, you know: pens in the pocket, works hard, talks smart, educated, etc. He comes from a family of citizens proudly doing their duty for America."

"Really?" James seems truly perplexed.

"Yes. His IQ is 145 and his dad was in the Coast Guard. Snowden was a CIA employee."

"CIA and they didn't listen to him?"

"He was a contract employee, maybe that's why. Not sure."

"Now he's a whistleblower and on the run. This is America, we are supposed to do the right thing, not protect our backs when not in our favor of the citizens if we wrong them." James couldn't help his altruistic side as it beamed forward.

"I know how you operate-this might be a good calling for you. But first the government has to get this worked out; they'll need a little time. The president will have to come on TV and down play it, and assure the Americans that it's all for the good of the country, and don't worry about a little spying-we have to get the bad guys. What he won't tell you is how we spied when you had a federal case, or stole your laptop, or followed your family intimidating them for fun."

"Meanwhile, we will slowly try and get a few of them ourselves, right here in America."

"Yup, that's us. Glad to have you James, and seriously, about this upcoming sting you will have back up. Just do your normal job protecting, and looking out. We'll have your back. Promise."

"I have to ask. Have they spied on Megan or Maria?"

"That's top secret. Sorry. Some things I can't tell you."

"I have a feeling. I think they did that's why this is so important. That's why I wasn't told, or else, I may have turned into an angry robot or gone AWOL."

"And we wouldn't want you to go AWOL. We don't want to lose valuable talent like you James."

And with that James knew but also knew he must stand tall and do the work. Consequences would come to those perpetrators of evil. "At least the man stopped what may have turned out to be the downfall of America."

"The story is still unfolding." Nate would not give out all the info that was his job. He had many working for him, going out and doing well. He knew he was young for this kind of work but he had been doing things alongside his dad for many years. He taught him.

After the two of them finish breakfast Nate pulls out the plan, shows it to him, and then shreds it. Simple as that.

"You ever hear from the lady with the tapped phone?"

"I've actually gotten in touch with her right before she was leaving the country."

"Lots of mysterious happenings occurring, I'd say."

"You got that right. And it all seems to be involving the hand held cell phone."

"1984."

"I never read the book." James thinks he should pick up a copy for him and Megan to read together.

"The real question is what are people doing with the information that they are receiving and to what benefit?'

"Obviously, the government has the upper hand upon the people and their daily freedoms. But it is also their job to catch the bad guys. There is going to be many a super sleuth out there I'm afraid. Let's get the bad guys first James."

"Roger that."

"I'm counting on you, as is Scarlet."

"What's next? Anything before my vacation at the lake house?"

"As a matter of fact," Nates laughs out loud, "the rest of your day is planned out before you get back and pack late this afternoon. This next meeting is highly confidential, take your own notes that only have meaning for you. You might not believe everything this person says but trust me I've verified the couple of notes she gave me. She doesn't have long to live, so spend the day, get everything."

"Is it necessary?"

"Absolutely, because she'll die and I need verification of her facts from you in closed chambers. That's why. She's the lady with the phone."

"So I get to meet the lady who left you her phone. These next three weeks are going to be questionable I have a feeling. I'll be checking my reality card ever so often. I may have to call you to be in touch."

"That's why I'm here to back you up. Always. Do well. This is important stuff that won't be let out in the open." Nate hands him a note to read. It's an address.

James says goodbye. He gets in his car, taps in the address, and then speeds away.

CHAPTER TWENTY SEVEN

James account of mysterious meeting...
The place isn't too far and once I pull up I can see it's a business. I take a second look and it's a hair salon. I check my phone before getting out of the car, Nate left a message and said have a nice lunch with Suzanne. I'm meeting Suzanne today. I'm actually very excited not knowing what I'm in for. This business had always been crazy-just seems like it really lifted off the ground lately. Everything is moving so fast, technology has gone haywire, and sir, you are right up there in the cloud with all this. Lucky me. For one last moment I think about Megan, my new love, and she puts a smile to my face, and all is well. I think we might even make a good team. We'll see. Most likely, I myself, am under someone's surveillance due to Megan and Maria. That's fine. Today, I look like I'm going to get my hair done and sit for a good shave. Except if I stay in here for five hours, well, someone may wonder why. I chuckle, let them wonder.

I get out of the car, leaving nothing behind as I know someone may case my car, bug my car, or put a tracer on it while I leave it. I scratch my day old growth allowing whomever is watching that I'll be going in for service-maybe they'll run out for coffee or lunch.

Once inside the lady at the front desk asks me if I can be helped.

"Yes, I'd like to see Suzanne."

"Sure, one moment please. Do you have an appointment?"

"I'm not sure, possibly, someone called for me."

"James?"

"Yes, that's me."

"Right this way, have a seat over here. I'll tell her you have arrived."

Nate, you are on the ball. You got me an appointment with Ms. Clue. Remember to take some notes, you might need them later on I remind myself. I grasp the outside of my shirt pocket, notes, pencil, and I'm ready.

"James," says a red-haired woman. We've been expecting you. Right this way. The shop is busy, bustling, and I am taken away, all the way to the back. Out through a secret back door we go, single file, through a bush lined path and we enter into the back door of a restaurant. I can smell the food, the spices, the pasta, the oregano, and bread.

"I guess we're eating an Italian lunch today." I whisper to myself. Is all this necessary? Must be.

I am led into a back room with three tables, very cozy, and no windows. She says, "Have a seat, Suzanne will be right in."

The scents from the bread have stirred my stomach which I ignore. I sit down and pull out my notes. I can't wait to meet her.

What I see next is not what I expected. A woman walks in with a large hat on over a scarf covering all of her head, large sunglasses, very dark sunglasses that is, and gloved arms with a warm up suit on.

"Hello, Mr. James," she says. "I am Suzanne, very nice to meet you." Her voice sounds a little frail.

"Hello, Suzanne, nice to meet you as well" I say. We shake hands but she doesn't look at me.

Acknowledging me to sit with her hand, I do, and she does the same. I notice she is very thin. Dying. Remember?

"Psychological water boarding," says Suzanne. That's a new term but an old trick for new tech.

I write that down. It seems important.

"Say what?" I question.

"You heard me, don't look at me though. And I won't look at you."

"Why is that?"

"I know it sounds crazy, doesn't it?"

"Extremely so," I add.

"Because then they will know who I've been to see. They have some special eye camera that records what I've seen. And if you are tagged then they'll see that you've seen me and I don't want to be seen. Though, now that I'm dying, it may not matter."

"Huh?" Her words immediately agitated me. She was talking like an expert. How would she know such things? I decide to listen up realizing as absurd as she may sound-someone has gotten to her. Either that or her pills have gone beyond the line of their duty.

"James, just listen to my truth, decipher it, and check it out. You got two to three hours, maybe four. Now ask away. Then, I'm gone for six months before I can see you again."

"Okay, beautiful, because I know you are … underneath all that disguise."

"I love flattery, pour it on."

We both smile and the interview is underway. The trust is there. The location is known to no one and the car surveilling mine is waiting, and waiting, and finally leaves for coffee, then returns, and waits some more.

"Suzanne, why don't you begin with why you dropped off your phone to my guy? Then tell me what your illness is, and how it's related; how this circumstance affected you, and finally, how can I help you, if at all?"

"First up, if you could have talked with me while this was going on you would have seen what bad shape I was in. I was scared right to the bone and I believe that was the intent to do that to me. I know it but I can't prove it. Even so I feel compelled to tell you, that you might find the perps then snuff them out. I just don't want it to happen to others. I feel for the children, or people that don't know any better about the internet. I didn't know. I was just learning. They taught me a lesson I can't get out of my head.

However, all things get better with time. I am better. Trust me it was horrible to think people are after you and it's not even the boogie man under the bed! It's real, there are real people watching you, following you in your own town."

"You are explaining the psychological waterboarding, your own term, I presume."

"Exactly. You are a quick study. Nate said I'd like you."

"I'm going to add here that you possibly felt like someone was garnering your trust, then tore it open like a wound, or made you feel insignificant or worried that they would get you in some fashion. They would kill you."

"How did you know?"

"I don't, except I was trained. Remember, I'm a seal and have Special Forces operations instructions, taught from the highest levels in America. I was taught how to break someone, repeatedly, if I wanted to."

"Except, I didn't think I signed up for that. All I did was join a few blogs, begin to get on Social Medias. There are so many, you know."

"Yes, I know. And the world is full of cameras and such."

"My son used to warn me and I just looked at him like, really?"

"You must be a very trusting person then."

"Yes, I am. I care about people. I'm a people person."

"How long has this been going on?"

"I'm a strong hold, in other words, when I start something I plan on finishing it. I started writing a book, always wanted to do that."

"A book? That seems like a nice thing to do, difficult I'm sure." I added.

"That's why I didn't leave my sites, even though, it seemed like I kept getting hacked. I changed passwords and kept writing, getting tips from online sources. The whole internet was breaking because traditional publishing was meeting social media and there was a firestorm of information. You could say it was the wild, Wild West of 2010. That's when I began."

"You've been at it a few years then?"

"I suppose, but it feels like seven."

"Why do you think you were targeted and fill me in on the waterboarding?"

"Let's just say they garnered my trust by helping with questions and encouragement, then a day later they walloped me good. They kicked me in the gut and destroyed whatever motivation I had by tearing down what they said previously. It doesn't make sense, I know. But thus I'm telling you-maybe it's a Chinese torture tactic, or possibly real forces were trained in this tactic to destroy me. Why? Well, I tried to figure that out."

"And what did you come up with?"

"A long time ago I assisted an attorney for this special case where this woman was obviously innocent but the guy was of high importance and they never wanted it to go to court. But when it did they tried everything to discredit her. They placed porn on her computer and tried to get her to download child porn. They were almost successful. But she wasn't into it, she liked politics, and would comment back and forth with others. She received a backlash the next day for her viewpoints and quit commenting further. She told me she received a scathing direct threat, scared her so much she thought she was going to die. She gave up."

"Why did this affect you?"

"Because I believed her. She was innocent. What are we doing to some women? We are not listening to them. We take them away, shut them up, and hope they never come back. I wanted to change that. Difficult to do by yourself."

"Yet you stayed online, changing your passwords, changing sites, and trying to trust others doing the same thing as you, writing books."

"Exactly. Once I figured out the psychological waterboarding tactic I tried not to be affected. It hurt me real bad. I persisted for that gal I met a long time ago. Internet bullies be damned I told myself and wrote more books."

"Good for you. It finally stopped?"

"I suppose they got tired of following me as I started new sites and started over."

"I am sorry you felt followed, stormed if you will, especially when you were trying something new. Do you remember the gals name so I can look up the situation?"

"Sure do. Victoria Red. She's a very dear lady but I don't think you'll find her-she went into hiding."

CHAPTER TWENTY EIGHT

I could see we were going to be talking all day. I asked her, "Do you mind if I record this conversation? I feel like you have some valuable information and I want to capture it correctly."

"Go ahead, it won't bother me except I hate my voice."

"Perfect. This way we can stop for lunch later, then pursue more."

"Sure," she nodded. We were sitting next to each other at the table but both either looking down or at the pictures on the wall. I could see her hat go up and down. In all my days this was most extraordinaire. I had a beautiful dame I couldn't see, only hear, and she had me mesmerized totally. Why? Because I think she knew more than she should have. She had a story to tell like no other I presumed.

"Let's start with the first date you noticed something because it's pretty standard to not know everything in the beginning. Then if you have to backtrack it will make more sense."

"Sure."

"I'm ready. Let's go."

"August 17th, 2010 sticks in my head as the date to remember. I can't seem to forget it. By that time I had had a very busy year already. I had been diagnosed with breast cancer stage three with six lymph nodes positive. I had two surgeries by June, and if that wasn't enough to throw at me I went and returned to school to get my RN licensure renewal. I spent all of May in school, an hour and a half away, followed by a test, and then did 160 hours of work in the Emergency Department at a local hospital. I paid an exorbitant fee of close to three thousand dollars to renew this license after working 24 years in nursing. Why I chose the year of my surgeries to do this I have no idea."

"Maybe being busy or the prospect of loss of life propelled you to go after what you wanted."

"Likely. I think at that point hearing the diagnosis, dealing with what to do, then going through the two surgeries with another one on the way, you are not really in charge of your life. You are just acting out the scenario. I turned to music, and the internet, I just did. No one in my family was going to comfort the nurse. I'm the comforter."

"Why August 17th?"

"I'd been on this site and it was fun, listening to music, and talking about movies, but it changed that day. It was weird, it was different, like someone new came aboard and shifted the whole plot. Also, around this time I decided not to do the third surgery, maybe I was tired from the whole year. I needed a break. I joined a few more Social Medias to keep abreast of the new technology to advise my daughter who has three children. I thought it so strange-like I kept getting hacked. One time when I was on a site handwriting came right over the site and drew on my computer. Seriously, like they were right in the room. Weird. Creepy. Look at my arms filled with goosebumps even with gloves on. It still gets me."

"Definitely creepy. Did you get your computer looked at or get some antivirus software?"

"Eventually, yes."

"I'll get on with your four questions. Why did I drop off the phone to Nate? Because it was driving me crazy. I did a very stupid thing when I was at school. See this is how trusting I am. Mind you this was a stressful time for me as my husband had died the previous year, and here I was, all alone combating this illness by myself."

"I'm so sorry."

"Thank you. I was sorry, too. On with it Suzanne ... Believe it or not someone befriended me there. Of course, I love talking and socializing, and one day we were sitting in our chairs in the back of the room. I was half there, daydreaming about my life, and had to use the restroom. She said, "Oh, leave your phone, I'll watch it. What do you think Ms. Trusty did? I left the phone and didn't think twice. I'm sure she bugged my phone. Why? I don't know. Why would anyone be interested in me and especially people from the law?"

"Any tickets, warrants, arrests, lawsuits, threats, drugs, DUI's, divorce, or run ins?"

"I'm as clean as a whistle, at least I thought so. It's my nature I don't like to be in trouble, so I follow the laws, well, one time I did get a speeding ticket and I was going very fast. Blame that on the car-it was meant to do that."

"Many people get a speeding ticket. Anyone in your family get in trouble with the law?"

"As a matter of fact there was but we lived states apart-so I didn't think it a problem."

"When did you recognize that maybe you were followed because of someone else?"

"Not at first-at all."

I could tell she was thinking about this and I gave her some time.

"My son who lives far away out west had a law suit or two against someone who had wronged him. I tried to stay out of it. And I did. My other son is the one who told me he had a felony and people in the upper branches of law seriously wanted him to stop going after them."

"All right, but these things are done in the court of law. So no worries."

"You would think that's how it goes, but most people know better, it's the attorneys who win cases, which is not always the truth."

"Okay, agreed. Back to you."

"This particular period of time over a few months is when he went missing, and then I think they came to look at me to see if I was harboring him. That makes sense, I get that."

"Were you?"

"No. Never."

At times, my conversation with others on the phone would be repeated back to me on the blog. Hacked again, though, after a while I figured someone is doing this to me to scare me. And they did scare me. How would you like it if every move you made was put back to you 24/7?"

"I honestly cannot imagine the horror." At this point my body shivers slightly for her, like if this was my mother I'd be so mad! I look at her hands in the gloves and she is shaking. The tremble will not stop.

"I took a little job and only worked a couple weeks. It was new to me this office work. The person in charge gave me a cup of coffee one day but was sure to pick it up after I had drunk it. This is speculation but I believe she wanted my fingerprints. Her husband did security work."

"That is speculation but I see how at this point you were becoming paranoid, and that just added to the situation and made it worse."

"Yes. Then I started reading and writing poetry. I was like a kid in a candy store. This woke me up, the written word, and I hadn't ever seen it as so beautiful. I suppose you could say I had an awakening. That is why I stayed with blogging and being on the internet, even though, I still got hacked. I changed passwords all the time. One time on a social media site-someone actually posted my password in a sentence while I was on. I know that many companies have had data breached. I just felt trolled or picked upon. It's unexplainable."

"Suzanne, I'm glad you are telling me. I want all of it."

"Thank you. There's more, that's only the beginning, the first six months anyway."

"I changed phones in January 2012 and if I had recognized my later thoughts about my school renewal for RN licensure, and my phone being tapped, I would have done it back in 2010. I didn't put two and two together until after Nate looked at it. He became suspicious and asked me if the camera ever turned on all by itself? I said yes, how did you know?"

"He's told me a couple people have had this complaint."

"I threw it against the wall and told him I don't want a phone. He could have it. He told me to come back, and I did visit him, and now I'm here with you."

"You okay to continue?"

"Yes, I'm good. They are bringing us some coffee and water, before lunch at eleven."

"When did it turn on? By itself anyway?"

"Crazy thing is it turned on at random periods but once when I was setting up a bath. Then I became extremely horrified!"

"Oh my, that's crazy!"

"Tell me about it. I want to look at you right now but I won't. I can imagine you wouldn't want that happening to anyone you know."

"Absolutely frightening, as though they have complete control over you."

"Thank you for your confirmation. I appreciate that. I knew I had to tell the right people."

"You have covered six months. I think we should keep going and fill me in on the little nuances, day to day, or big occurrences over the next year, 2011."

"I need to mention that after one of my surgeries I needed another bottle of pain meds, and after I picked these up in the drive through I went to another drug store to get other supplies. When I came out there was a car facing me with the guy at the steering wheel staring straight at me. He looked like he was on business. He pulled out, made haste, and sped away. Another person was at a store and kept following me around watching what I was purchasing. Once I told my daughter I thought they were following me because of their missing brother. She couldn't believe it either. Then it slowed down, then there was nothing. I thought reprieve. Yeah."

We pause.

"I hid my phone in the dresser one time so it couldn't tell me what I was doing. But one time I said to myself this is 1984, and I'm in it. Mind you my insides were being pummeled, knowing someone was watching me at all times. This scared the shit out of me. Pardon me, there are no better words. But see then they let me know they were watching me. I thought maybe it was the mob-maybe the mob is smarter than all our forces put together. What came to mind was how a juror is swayed. I can see how they can get to someone. I know I was gotten to, by being shaken and stirred, until I was half crazy."

"Suzanne, this is just plain wrong and should not be a part of our democracy."

"I know that."

"I'm listening."

"One time I was getting dressed in my closet and looked over at my plum outfit debating if I should wear it or not. Later on, sure enough, someone I follow who was nice and writing poetry like me had a plum outfit on. I thought okay this must be Photoshop, but why? Why threaten me or horrify me and be this weird? I actually looked up at my ceiling, my clothes, everywhere looking for bugs. The only thing that I could come up with was this couple I let come in and look around as I was getting ready to sell my house. I had let them in and the guy went on his own tour whereas the woman stayed with me. Who were they really? I honestly don't know. My neighbor was with me that day so I wasn't scared. You see, too many strange occurrences. What do I have to do to get away from this? And what do they want? Don't know if it was CIA or FBI? I sound like a looney tune."

"I want to find out what they want. Badly. I believe you, honey."

"You do?" Her voice cracked.

"Yes."

CHAPTER TWENTY NINE

"Thank God. Because I believe myself but every now and then I say, seriously Suzanne, shake it off. But I know better because this never happened to me in my life before. The clothing thing was a real breaker. What I figured out from that was they wanted to scare me and they used a nice person's account to do it."

We both pause a minute and take a deep breath. For the first time I notice the pictures on the wall which is not like me. I'm supposed to know everything all at once. It's a picture of a waiter I suppose in France out on the streets. Such a simple job, a simple life. One day I will have that after I figure out who the fuck has bothered this beautiful lady who hasn't bothered anyone.

"One more thing while I'm talking about that couple. She told me he had to go to Alabama for the weekend. The next day someone was killed in Alabama mysteriously. So that was someone trying to get my goat or scare me again. Why on earth the terror? It was like terrorism. Someone has figured out how to terrorize people over the internet. Terrorism." She shakes her head.

"Terror is a good word. It can be learned. Did you think it was possibly coming from overseas?"

"I don't know. It was at times subtle, then other times,

forcibly in my face, and it didn't stop. This was not about helping me like with the writer helping me to form a poem, no this was trolling and through the use of Social Media. Yet they had to be inside my home-now that is the terrifying part."

"Are you tired yet?"

"No. Oh, look here's our coffee and water coming in. Thank you." She set down the coffee for both of us and then left the room.

"In late 2011 I had the final surgery and then completed chemotherapy. I also had it out with my daughter. Our relationship became estranged during this time. Believe me, I thought maybe it was the chemotherapy playing with my brain cells. One time when online I saw something that resembled an old doctor's bag, something she would have talked about with her husband. I asked her if she had talked about this recently, she thought so but she also thought I was way off board with my thoughts and discoveries. She said it couldn't be so and dismissed me. I thought maybe she had signed me up for online counseling or something. It just seemed that way, you know. She used to send me coupons from the internet and even those had a mysterious message."

"Tell me about that."

"Well coupons are supposed to help you find something low cost. Sounds good. But connected to that coupon was a news release with a date and time, and it was as though you received the news ahead of time, not when the general public received it. Also, it contained other important information not a regular person would know like police information. I kid you not. I'm weird, I know. But I'm telling the truth. Seriously, someone wanted me. Someone had it out for me, I just know it."

"1984 Suzanne. I'm so sorry."

"Thank you. Do you understand how I could not go to the police, et all?"

"I do understand. Because you thought it was them terrorizing you."

She broke down and had to use a napkin for her eyes underneath the sunglasses. She was still paranoid from real circumstances. This was new. We don't usually terrorize our own citizens. I give her time and I drink some coffee. I am especially glad I decided to tape this. Where was I going to hide these tapes and who could I trust with these? Anybody could have threatened her from anywhere. But I had some likely culprits and ideas.

"Sorry, it still gets me what I let happen. I should have stopped but there really was nice people teaching me to write poetry and learn my English all over again for prose and novels."

"You did not let anything happen! This is not your fault!" I almost shouted. I had my course in equality, and how women can be abused because they are, the nice ones, the trusting ones, the caring, or nurturers.

"Yes. I know. But hey we are taught to say that from an early age. Not every guy understands like you. We all should not have to be so tough. Some are sensitive and giving, that's all right in my book."

"How did the surgery go and the rest of 2011?"

"The surgery went well, and I was glad I had it. I think we should have lunch. I'm saving some good stuff for you for after I eat. You ready?"

"Sure. Where to?"

"I'll call the ride. These days I take a limo-they drive me wherever I want. I know a place out of the way and the car tracking you won't find us."

"How do you know?"

"Because I've trained my stylists to be very observant, and they report everything back to me." She laughed. She deserved it.

Next thing I knew we were being huddled out through another door, and on our way to her place, Suzanne's out of the way place. Once in the limo I sit back and enjoy the ride. I try not to look at her and her the same. This is a first.

"To answer number three question, *'How is this related to my illness?'* Actually, I just don't know. I believe someone was trying to help me overcome this dreaded disease with tips on nutrition, exercise, etc. but then I was thinking how does anyone even know I have it. I barely told anyone, just my friends, and didn't post it to Social Media. At that time I had like ten friends on Social Media, and I think I kept it private. What I realized was my private information was leaked, my very own personal healthcare information. That is against the law. Others should not have your private health report. It's a federal offense, actually. We were taught as nurses to never give out info, especially when we had a famous patient."

"And this bothered you?"

"Bothered me? I'm a nurse, we protect people's privacy. That's a no-no and has been for a long time. I've taken care of people, priests, lawyers, doctors, and the general public. We don't talk. Period. I take that very seriously! I'm by the book for the most part."

"When the abominable happened to you what did you do?"

"That's question number four."

"After lunch then?"

"Ha. No let me answer that and then after lunch I'll give you six more items to ponder."

She paused. I waited. This was getting real good. I began to think that I could make a home based business out of this. Megan could help me, be the actress to get the goods, all right here in the good old US of A.

"What did I do and how did it affect me?"

Suzanne removed her hat and I saw it on her lap. A scarf covered her head I could tell from the corner of my eye. The driver slowed as he drove on a country road.

"I didn't do anything because I thought people were after me, I gaged it, watched it, and couldn't believe it. Maybe it was all in my head, maybe it was a huge hoax. Except it wasn't. I feared for my life thinking someone was going to kill me like some people in high places have people killed, knocked off cause they know too much. *The evil deeds of the rich and powerful is what* I thought. That pissed me off, and I said to myself, how dare someone get away with running over the little guy? It's not fair. I live in America and I'm a citizen. I obey the laws; they should too. Who appointed them to destroy the lives of underlings?"

"Why don't you run for Congress or the Senate? I'm serious."

"How sweet. Love to. But I got to cure this shitty disease with more poison for a few months."

"Somehow, I don't think it's over. By that I mean your life."

"Sweet again. You need to be somebody's baby, James."

After a few moments…

"James it affected me so much I nearly caved. I tried to talk with people around me by telling them they didn't believe me. I couldn't get anyone to listen. I had to do it alone. I was not on drugs-though, I sound like I am. I felt like they were coming at me from three sides. They were in my car, my house, on my computer, following me everywhere and I thought it disgusting. I thought it the biggest fraud and abuse of power I ever heard of. At first I thought maybe a nonprofit was trying to help but it progressed into more than that. I just did my daily routine and kept my wits about me with an occasional big eyed, eyebrow raising "Oh. My. Gosh. What's next?"

"I don't use a phone now; I don't want to be traced and tormented."

"So the problem is solved?"

"No it's not over. But soon I hope. Am I coming back from these dark times, the crazy cancer and all its doom and gloom? Probably. But I want someone like you to know about this to prevent this strange occurrence from happening to others. Get the bad guys and lock them up, not the good people that raise a hand and try to keep our freedoms."

"I believe I can help you and I know I can get the bad guys because they always do it again. Crooks are crooked and they can't control themselves."

"Oh, look, here we are."

Suzanne puts her hat back on and I look out the window. I think we are at a vineyard in North Georgia.

"Monteluce Winery."

The conversation at the vineyard would have nothing to do with her situation-she insisted. We were in public; we chatted, laughed, drank wine, and enjoyed an exquisite lunch.

CHAPTER THIRTY

We both take a short nap on the way back and when we arrive to the villa restaurant in town we shuffle back into the little table room with scenes of Italy on the walls.

"Thank you for such a fine lunch. I enjoyed it. It was delicious."

"You're welcome."

"How much time do you have left?"

"I think we'll conclude in about one hour. Anything I miss I'll tell you this Christmas or maybe next summer. Sound good?"

"Perfect. Proceed."

"This will be succinct. Better turn that recording on."

Suzanne pulled out a little piece of paper with her own notes on it. "I do get forgetful. Trying to remember everything that happened over three years can be tough."

"For sure."

"I took three trips over last year in 2012, one to Vegas and two to Florida, and they are memorable. I love to go gambling but more for the excitement of the nightlife, games, shows, entertainers, dinner, shopping not so much but sitting by the pool is so lovely. They even have spas so you can party at night and feel pampered during the day.

My girlfriend and I went to Vegas and one morning I found myself eating breakfast alone. Well, of course, you know I wasn't alone. Sure enough I looked around and spotted someone eyeing me. They were reading a paperback and watching me. I'm not really worth it but because all these shenanigans were going on I said to myself. Jesus, Mary and Joseph, hell yes, this is bigger than me. I knew then it was bigger than me. How big I did not know?"

I have to chuckle. "At least you had a sense of humor about it."

"It troubled me a little and I looked around my room for any bugs. But you see I didn't know what a bug looks like. On that same trip we went to the top of one of the IT places. The patio was outside at the top of the world. One could see everywhere in all directions. I was followed there too."

"How on earth did you know?"

"Easily. A guy who worked there went past me and purposely bumped into me so hard it made me turn around and lose my balance. I think he was cuing his cohorts in security that I was here. You might think I have a big ego, but I don't. I paid attention because all these strange things were happening. They were out of the ordinary. I thought maybe my son really pissed someone off or something, or that the government seriously had it out for him by watching me. I know I was probably mistaken on this account but I had no other clues or couldn't think of a reason on earth that people were interested in me."

"You just knew and were paying attention to the clues presented. Smart woman."

"Thank you."

"On the first trip to Florida and on down to the Bahamas with my same friend, we stopped in south Florida and went shopping. I picked out many items, that's how I shop. I went to pay and lo and behold the dude looked at me like I was some crook right after he swiped my credit card. He looked at me again and went to get his boss. They both looked at me and worked on the processing but eyeing me the whole time I was in the store. I felt like they thought I was a shoplifter or something. In actuality, after I left I said to myself I bet my credit card is tagged, traced or whatever they do to see what someone buys. Good God, maybe I was paranoid. Please find out that I wasn't, it might ease my mind. And if I am sane-then it will make for a good thriller or suspense novel."

"All these items scared you for your safety. They gave you pause to question your validity, sanity, and possible life ahead for you."

"James, well spoken." I find this lady to be well spoken herself, alert, and quick. She was smart, not paranoid.

"The third trip this year was earlier in June. I went with my daughter and her kids to the beach, on the Gulf. We stayed at a lovely place and even played golf. We had to take a golf cart to get over a bridge and go to the beach. I enjoyed this tremendously. But the very first day we arrived and parked the car there was a jeep right next to our spot, a black jeep just like one I used to have when I was young. Only certain people would know this, not everyone knows this detail. Okay, I can live with a black jeep, no problem. But when I got out of our car and looked at the large place card with the name on it. Guess what?"

"Ah, it was your first name?"

"No. Guess again?"

"I don't know." I swallow. This is sounding very evil and purposeful. I think I know what is going to come next and this is a tactic used to water board individuals. With purpose. Knowingly terrorizing an individual to get them to be afraid. Fear. Knowing.

"You know don't you. This is bad shit. Evil."

"I'm guessing it is your last name, your maiden name, something only a few would know. Not likely a coincidence. Done for fear."

"There was my last name on the card in the slot next to us on a vehicle I use to own. Talk about being followed. I panicked but kept it to myself."

"Terror."

"My heart skipped beats but I couldn't alert my daughter and ruin her vacation. She would have told me to get a life, quit being preoccupied. I thought if someone wanted to kill me they would have. At this point. It became real. They had me. Badly."

"Why would someone go through all this trouble to frighten you? I'm sure you asked yourself this question over and over."

"I did but couldn't come up with anything except the son on the lamb. But he was caught and went to jail. So all said and done. It should have gone away but it didn't. It persisted."

"And."

"I knew my house was rigged, like every room spoke to me, not literally. When I would get on my Social Medias or even my phone, weird things occurred. I finally figured out that the smoke detectors had the goods. That's how they watched me. Once again why would anyone want to watch me? Or torture me?"

"Did they break down?"

"How did you know?"

"Because they were cheap or whatever?"

"Not sure, but one month they all fell apart and my son

came to replace them. They all fell apart at once."

"Interesting."

"Another thing when my grandkids come to do homework and send it across the wire to their teachers they never get it. My house, the internet anyway, doesn't work properly. Job applications, homework, and other things don't go through. It's as though someone is deciding what can go through my line. They've had people out to look at our neighborhood but we've accepted that it just works slowly at times. A coworker of mine had all her belongings stolen right from her house in town. She said three others on the same street had stuff stolen. She thinks the cops are in on it. I think maybe its security-they know when you are there or not. She said they never found her things, and likely a big truck came and loaded it up and then gone just as fast. What is this world coming to?"

"I should read that book, 1984. Have you read it?"

"No, maybe I should. Maybe I'll find my answers in there. But I feel pretty strong about this James. Nate said you would help. I hope you can."

"Finally, tell me has it stopped and when did it stop? And how can I help you?"

"It has stopped. My son lives with his sister and it seems to be over. I think his troubles are through, finished."

"When did it stop?"

"The day he was released."

"How can I help you?"

"I received a call a year ago, an anonymous caller, and they said my truths should be told. So here I am telling you."

"Why did you believe the caller?"

"Why not?"

I smiled. I think we are done. I look at the wall again. I feel sorry that this elderly lady had to endure an illness, then a surveillance, followed by cyber terror, and have nothing left but a punched in the gut feeling. She was right. I needed to make sure this doesn't happen to others. She was also right in that she was more attuned because her son had been in trouble with the law. But if I could help it I would get to the bottom of this, with Nate's help, and preserve our freedoms and keep them intact. We didn't need to be harassing witnesses or good people just because they were related or knew something.

"One more question?"

"Why not tell a reporter or paper?"

"Because my other son tried that years ago and it failed."

"I see."

"I trust you."

"Thanks."

I give her my hand and we shake, then she gives me a hug. "Good luck. Hope to see you again, then you can see all of me."

"Looking forward to that."

That was it. Done. Fin.

We left and I did hope to see her again. I hope I will have terrific news for her. I just found a new motivation to add to my new relationship.

CHAPTER THIRTY ONE

I head home to pack and ready myself for some R & R. Megan's point of view ...

We arrive at the lake house but when we knock on the door and insert the key, we immediately realize we have arrived at the wrong place. We get back into the car and go up and down the street again. Finally, we find it and can't believe it will be our place. It's bigger than I expected and it has a pool. James didn't know this either. What a plus! We exit the car and walk around the side before trying the key.

"James, the pool is divine and it comes with a diving board. Unbelievable!"

"The boys are going to love this. We will have to watch them when they are out here so there isn't any pushing and shoving." James looks all around and then we retreat back to the car to unload our belongings.

"Grandma and Grandpa bring them tomorrow at ten o'clock in the morning."

James gives me a big hug, "We have the place to ourselves tonight."

"Tomorrow, I'll take the kids with me to the grocery store while you set everything up and running, boats and all."

"That sounds like a plan. We can order pizza tonight,"

he added.

We go inside and tour around this mansion. There were cedar beams inside that stretched across the ceiling from end to end. Many of the walls were made out of logs. It had that log cabin type feel with an enormous fireplace in the center of the room just off the kitchen, and one just outside through the glass doors to a covered stone terrace. I thought for a moment that maybe we should invite some friends up for a weekend, then remembered James said this is part business. The views out to the lake were out of a picture book. Quite serene.

"Boy is this going to be fun!" He comes up behind me and twirls me around. I smile and close my eyes. All of this is for us. We won't ever want to go back home. I felt special right in the here and now.

We play around some more and take our suitcases up to the master bedroom. Of course, it is glorious, comfortable, and with a stunning view that looks out onto the lake framed by some tall trees. We unpack and use the dressers provided, then step into the bathroom. How could a bathroom be this luxurious at a lake? But it was and I unpack my toiletries thinking I had just arrived into a five star hotel in some glitzy city and not out here on a lake near the woods with an intimate cabin feel.

We were going to have three glorious weeks here with three days for my boys. I would have to watch them as this had some serious obstacles like a pool, a lake, boats, and jet skis. One thing for sure I knew they would be sleeping like babies come nightfall. I suppose there will be fireworks on the Fourth and a picnic. I need to buy that food tomorrow. I head down to the kitchen to make a plan and look through the cookbooks for a couple recipes. I was only twenty seven and still rely on recipes, not having everything memorized in my head. Also, I wanted to try new things all the time. James joins me in the kitchen to pull out the frozen pizza-courtesy of the owners, and find the bottle of wine.

"Tell me some things you like to eat at picnics."

"Whatever you want to make. I can't wait to eat what you cook."

"Seriously, you are ready to try my food, even things I've never made?"

"I'm game. We're on vacation!"

I pull out Betty Crocker, Better Homes & Garden, and The Lady and Sons from Savanna and begin to scatter through the pages, looking for hot dishes to please my new mate, hoping I'll make a good impression.

"Here's one, Cowboy Salad, which sounds delish and easy. What do you think?"

"I said, anything you want, I'll eat. I do like baked beans, grilled meat, and pie."

"What kind of pie?"

"Cherry, apple, or even strawberry," he said.

"Strawberry sounds very good and healthy. Let me look." I began writing down page numbers and ingredients after selecting a menu. This was fun. I didn't get to do this at home as much of the time I worked or it seemed like I was running from one job to another picking up the boys, doing laundry, grocery shopping, etc. But now I get to have a handle on this. I can be a mom and enjoy the journey. I could hear a talk show host saying those words. But in real life, it didn't creep like a turtle's pace, it jumped and snuck around like a lizard, then definitely ran like a race horse crossing the finish line. Except there was no finish line. I could see where four hands were better than two but my ex and I did not make it work, it was harder for us to be together. It just was. Sad. When I was twenty five and the twins turned five he looked at me and said, 'I'm sorry. I can't do this.'

I remember looking back at him and I agreed; he wasn't cut out for it and hadn't been a part of the family since the twins turned two. Was I? Well, I had no time to think, just do. And so I did. I had always wanted kids, maybe not three so close in age, but my own family was happy and I wanted to repeat that.

Now fast forward two years and here I am. Dating. I waited over two years with one year divorced and the first person I date I fall in love with. Was this luck or what? I didn't know as yet but I think this little trip to the lake might tell both of us. And the idea of a new career for me sounds intriguing. I look up to find Mr. Hot and Handsome looking at me.

"What sort of meat do you like to grill?" I ask James.

"Me? I like lean steaks and chicken. I'm sure your boys eat hot dogs and hamburgers, right?"

"Yes, and they like pasta but not potato salad, as yet. They don't like the mayonnaise dressing. My mom said I was the same way until I got older. I can make both. Maybe we can skewer shrimp and pineapple." I looked up again and James was very close.

He kisses me, for a long time.

"It will all taste very good, but you taste the best."

I set the list down on the counter. "Let's go down on the dock while the pizza cooks for a quick look around."

James pours me a glass of wine and we wait to put the pizza in for when we return. Good idea I think.

We stroll down to the dock and sit out on the end with our feet in the water as the lake becomes calm and wave less. The stillness had settled in and we reflect on a few things; we slowly talk about the future while we sip our wine. This feels right. This feels good.

The next morning at ten I meet the kids at the grocery store in town where the grandparents drop them off to me. I thank them and say, "I'll bring them back to you on July 5th." I hug them then say, "The boys are so lucky to have you guys in that you want to be with them and play a little. I love it and so do they."

CHAPTER THIRTY TWO

I know people stare at me and wonder why on earth I would bring three boys into the grocery store? I'm used to it by now; I've had seven years of practice. You do what you must. Do people know how hard it is to raise little ones? I'm sure they do but when I get stares you'd think it's the first time they've seen a human being under the age of fifteen.

I learned back in the beginning after my divorce that you just have to muster through all the shit, day after day. Because they have to learn at some point to be quiet, observe, and help their mother. I trudge in with one helping me push while one sat in the seat, and the other, the seven year old led the way. I had my list in hand and was able to maneuver through the store with minimal excitement or interruption. They were excited to see the lake house. I told them if they were good in the store-I'd let them have Doritos on the way home. I told them I had a surprise when we got to the car that I couldn't wait to tell them. This is how I dealt with kids, small little bribes to occupy them that I kept, and rewarded them, for good behavior.

As we were exiting the store this man walks in, he vaguely looks familiar. Actually, not familiar, just very strange. He had a cold dark stare which did not go unnoticed by myself. He was extremely skinny with shaggy, dirty blonde hair. And he stares back at me. Ouch. I look away and head right for the car. He gave me goosebumps and I thought next time I need to go to another store because, frankly, at the moment I feel uncomfortable about my safety and for my kids. I leave in a hurry. Call it sixth sense or whatever. Maybe my new line of business was instilling a sense of questioning, reasoning, or always looking for clues around me. I thought this location was safe but maybe not.

"Thanks guys for being good in the store."

I look back and I see my seven year old give me a thumbs up. I smile.

"Guess what?"

"Tell us momma!"

I couldn't help but smile ear to ear.

"The lake house has a pool!"

"A pool? Great!" They all shout. The oohs and aahs lasted a good while. Smiles too.

"And guess what else it has?"

"Whaaaaat?"

"A diving board for jumping off into the water."

I look back and I could see high fives, over and over, followed by the word, yes, spoken from their lips. Yes, the pool would be a hit!

Once we got there the boys ran to the back and I head in with the groceries to the kitchen. Pretty soon they come running in to get their suits on. "Okay, here's the rule. Someone must be out there watching you, myself, or James. Period. Or you get grounded. Got it?"

"Okay. Can you come out as soon as you get the groceries put away momma?"

"Sure. Give me fifteen minutes."

The boys enjoy the swimming pool. Likely that's all they needed but before dinner we ask them to come to a small park to go for a walk.

The boys run ahead on the wide trail. James and I talk some more about the future. I told him about the incident at the store and he assures me that the store is visited by some country folk but safe.

"Still, trust your instincts. Observe and try to put things in a logical sequence of these observations."

"My own private teacher. I love it." I squeeze him and give him a hug. Then when I stop and look ahead I see a man who looks as though he is from India focused on me. He has his phone out in front of him and he was snapping pictures. I look behind me to see if there was something interesting. The only thing interesting was James and I, I determine. I look at James. No way could I tell him this or he would think me nuts. I didn't tell him. But I was certain and when we pass each other I look at the man and he stares at me, he did not scowl, smile, or laugh. He just looked at me like in amazement, like he'd seen a ghost. Okay, I tell myself learn to put observations in logical sequence.

I had enough for one day. I was ready to go home, watch a movie or read a book.

I lay my head down and right before I fall asleep my mind decides to tango with the recent events. What do they mean? James says trust your instincts, put these observations in a logical sequence. That is exactly what I do but it doesn't make sense. I try again. The guy at the store was creepy, just plain creepy, and he stared at me with cold black eyes. Cold black eyes, where have I seen those? I ask myself. Suddenly a chill goes through me. I know. I know. Prison. I've never been to prison myself but I did visit it once. In college I took this course about law, and we ended up visiting a correctional facility, not just any old jail, but a federal lockup for hardened criminals, the worst of the worst. Basically, it's sad to say but these guys are almost like animals, they have gone beyond your basic drug dealer, auto theft, bank robbery, and they had cold black eyes with hardened stares that didn't really look at you. We had to write a paper and that's what I wrote about-the "Cold Black Eyes."

I lay there with my own eyes shut and go through the observations. I see a guy with cold black eyes staring at me, then later a dude snapping photos of me looking like he'd seen a ghost. I would say he took my picture purposefully, like he knew who I was. But why? The old question we always retreat to. Why? I reflect back on the other incidents. The big guy who came storming into my house, looking at my children, the two guys who tapped my line whom I later saw at the park, then of course, the call for Maria to the marble place by the river, and the cop who shot his girlfriend to save my life. If somebody really wanted me dead, I'd be dead. So they don't want me dead, they want something or someone near me. Maybe. James said Maria must be the target and I'm one of her best friends. What does she have that they want? This is where James tells me to just be quiet and let it all play out. We'll get the bad guys; we'll find them. Usually, money is involved, James tells me. Maybe though its electronics I tell myself and the potential for what knowledge it could uncover. I open my eyes. That's it! I know it. But I'm not an investigator as yet. I'm in training.

I look out the window and see the moon. It's almost full. I bet tomorrow, the 4th of July will be a full moon. I'm looking forward to tomorrow. I turn in bed and decide to go to sleep as I cannot figure out any more sleuthing tonight. Tomorrow will be perfect and I look forward to seeing how James and the boys play together. This idea makes me smile. I drift off into deep slumber.

CHAPTER THIRTY THREE

I'm up before the sunrise and set out to the kitchen to begin baking all the tempting dishes I've planned for on this special day in America here on the lake. The Fourth of July is always fun, kids love it. I bake the pies first, I settle on two, and then go for the side dishes of cowboy salad, baked beans, corn on the cob, tator tot casserole, the burgers, and a couple of dips for the chips. I decide to make a punch like the picture on a magazine cover. It has strawberry juice, kiwi juice and ginger ale; it just looks refreshing and good for the kids. Also, I have lemonade and ice tea with ginseng and lemons for the rims. These should last us the whole three weeks! The strawberry pie looks delicious, apple does too. We are having the hot dogs and burgers for lunch and the chicken breasts for dinner with barbeque sauce and con queso cheese over top to go with our cowboy salad. I set out the plates and napkins and donuts for breakfast. Then I make the coffee and go sit on the couch and read my book. The life of a mom on vacation I think to myself. This thought makes me think I've died and gone to heaven. I think possibly I may have.

That is until I see the police car out front in the neighbor's driveway. What? I get up and peer through the window-then run to get James in the bedroom.

"James, you're up? Good. There's a police car in the neighbor's driveway. Is that part of the plan?" I ask.

"No, that would not be part of the plan." He walks out the bedroom door and goes to the front of the log home. He sees the patrol car and an officer heading for the front door.

I am a bit worried. James goes to get dressed. "Let's eat breakfast, then I'll find out what happened."

I tell my worried self, *snap out of it*. It's nothing.

Everyone is up and out the door with a donut in hand. They head for the dock to play and find some fish. I set myself down there to watch over the happy crew. My eight year old looks down and decides the end of the dock would be a good place to jump off. He takes a running leap into the air. The others wait to see him pop up from underneath the water. The two of them, the twins, decide to wade in from the shore and meet him out where they can still touch. They all know how to swim but are not taking any chances. I've brought the sunscreen and tell them thirty minutes without then everyone gets a dose of prevention.

"All right momma!" He screams as he runs and jumps off the dock. I know the twins want to-they just aren't ready yet. But I bet by noon they will be ready.

James joins us and tells us he will take us for a boat ride before lunch. "How does that sound?"

"Sure thing."

"I'll be right back with the life jackets and floats. The tube is already on the boat."

"Remember the tube a couple weeks ago?" I ask my crew.

"Yes, that sounds great. I'll go first."

"Of course you will!" I say. "Will you guys do that?"

"Okay, maybe mom will try it. Do you have water skis?"

"Sure do. You can do that, no problem."

"Okay. I will. You boys can go one at a time with me to try it out if you like."

"How do we do that?" Asks the youngest.

"You will stand right in front of me and I'll lift you out."

"I'll do that." They both chime in.

After a while James anchors the boat and the kids go in to float or swim in the water. We are tucked away in a cove all by ourselves. The kids have life jackets on so we can rest easy for a few minutes.

I pass the chips to James and ask him what he wants to drink. The sun is up and it's hot outside. "I'll take a bottled water."

"Here you go."

"Thanks. The neighbors place was broken into last night."

"Really?"

"Really. They were not home. They were out for the evening."

"Is that part of the plan?"

"No Megan that was not part of the plan."

"Are we safe? Are my boys safe?"

"Yes, we are protected. And nothing happens until tomorrow."

"Except it did. It already did." I stare into James's eyes and cannot look away. I need him to reassure me more. Can he do that? He looks away. He can't. I don't know why.

"I trust my superiors. It's a simple as that."

"Then, I'll trust you. For now."

After lunch we use the jet skis, me on one and James on the other. The twins go with James and my oldest comes with me. We go and circle the lake, not too fast, just enough to catch our own wake quite a few times. We are the cool ones today, James and I. By mid-day we all need to get out of the sun for a while. Everyone takes a little nap and when the boys get up they help James collect some wood for a bonfire tonight. There's a fire pit and that will work very well. I set the table and use a paper tablecloth I bought with special plates and cups. I even blow up a couple balloons for the evening picnic. As I take out some trash I find myself staring over at the neighbor's house. I would have invited them but they are going to a friend's house for a picnic who also lives on the lake. They go by boat James tells me. He reassures me we are safe. I want to believe him but after the Rebekka incident with triple murders how can I believe in any safety?

It's a quiet night filled with sparklers before the fireworks take off a half hour later. One can see many families filling the sky with store bought replicas of big events. It is fun to sit there with our bonfire as our chairs circle the fire pit and everyone is happy. We feel like a big happy family on this night of our countries celebration. It is what I always wanted, lots of kids and a happy, handsome husband. I look over at James, maybe I will get that in the end. I don't know but right now it feels like I have it.

"I'll go get dessert and bring it out here by the fire." I leave the one big happy family for a few moments.

CHAPTER THIRTY FOUR

We all sleep in past our usual wake up times. It is July 5th, I go rouse the boys as I'll have to take them to the grandparents at noon. When I open the door to the room they are watching television in bed. The boys begin laughing and pointing at the set. I look over and there are three older teens or twenty somethings vomiting onto the floor right on top of their pizza.

"What is happening?"

"I don't know mother but these idiots are vomiting on the pizza they just had delivered. Is that supposed to be funny?" My oldest asks me.

"Are they going to eat it?"

My big eyes give it away and I add, "That is gross. Stupid and gross. Why are you watching this?"

"It's not even funny," says Patrick.

I turn the channel but not before the boys on TV look into the camera and laugh, then step into their own vomit. I should get channel blocking; I'll have to ask Phil Yeatling this when I get home. He's my neighbor and knows all about TV stations and which ones are appropriate. Then again he is probably off on some sailboat with a gal he met on the internet. He liked to do that, that and drink wine. He made documentary movies too. Maybe he made this movie with his son. For what reason I couldn't think of except to annoy someone.

"I want the Disney channel or the Science channel."

"I want the movie channel."

"I brought a couple videos for you all to watch. Let me go get one."

"Okay mom. When do we leave?"

"In about two or three hours."

I take my boys to meet Grandma and Grandpa. I am sad but then realize I will be very busy with James. Firrst up, though, I pick up a prescription for myself. My birth control would run out before I leave, so I pull up and use the drive up window. I hand the lady attendant my prescription and she said it would be about fifteen minutes. I pull away and go around back to wait out the time. Then I see Grandma and Grandpa; they have arrived early. Good.

I send my boys on their way and wait another five minutes before pulling up to the drive thru. When I pull up I see a guy on a hand held radio with long curly blond hair-looking around. He looks at me and then ducks out of view. What the fuck? Seriously. Do I have horns on my head or what? I tell myself in this world of what the hell's, plan on a few more of them. James better have some darn good answers and explain to me what world I stepped into. I thank her for the prescription-no more babies for a while.

By the time I get back to the log home there is another car parked on the gravel path. I assume our company has arrived. James did tell me he was doing a favor for a friend and letting her son come for a night or two with his girlfriend. They probably wouldn't be much trouble and do their own thing for the most part. James said we could eat the leftovers and go out for dinner to The Lodge tomorrow night with them.

I see the girl come out and get something from the car. "Nice car. I'm Megan."

"Thank you. Its sweet for sure, rides like a dream. Know what I mean?"

I extend my hand and she takes notice, but doesn't offer hers. "I'm Carmen." She smiles and winks at me.

We walk inside and there's the boyfriend. "Hello, I'm Angel. Great to meet you. James has been telling me all about you, and your boys."

"Yes, nice to meet you as well. I'm Megan."

"We are headed to the dock if you'd like to come."

"I'll pass for now but be out there later."

"Same here. Enjoy yourself. You know how to operate a boat?" Asks James.

"I don't but she does. We'll be fine."

"Later." Carmen grabbed her fellow by the arm and pulled him along. They practically ran to the dock.

"Okay, here I am." I say.

"Come here, you wonderful woman. Join me, follow me."

Needless to say I comply without hesitation. I lock the door. I want no surprises from Carmen, the friendly woman, or anyone else at the moment.

Even though we have company outside down at the dock I'm not in any way disturbed. My boys are safe and I am in love. I give James all of my attention. No dinner to cook for two days. I am so ready for this afternoon in bed. In fact, I think to myself the couple that came to visit will be a nice distraction tonight, and then back to my lovely James.

James is tan except for his bottom and I stare as he walks around closing the blinds and curtains. I find a candle to light and turn on the bedside radio. It's a no go. James has his speaker and uses blue tooth off of his phone. This momentarily makes me think of all the phone mess of late.

Quickly, though, I ignore it.

The room is quiet except for the low volume of James playlist. I feel like we are all alone and no one in the entire world cares what we are doing at this moment. It's been a long time since I've felt cared about, touched, or loved. I lay back and watch James come over to the bed. We are naked and each of us is anticipating the others kisses and love.

We kiss and lay with each other for an eternity right here in this enclosed shelter from the world. I am free and emotionless except for the smile on my face that won't stop with this venture. I am in the middle of pure ecstasy. No one is tugging at me, shouting at me, nor yelling 'mommy.' I kiss him with all of me and our bodies heat up as we touch and hold one another. He gathers my hair and places it behind my ear and looks deep into my eyes as only he can. That stare is taking me somewhere else and I shall let it.

"I love you Megan."

"I love you James."

We take a shower and save our energy for later tonight. James says it's time for a boat ride around the lake and to make our guests feel welcome.

"Let's bring the leftovers and some beers on the boat. We can stop and eat before the sun sets out there on the lake," I recommend.

"Perfect."

We gather up a picnic and tell our guests the plan. They like the idea. We all head down to the boat around 6:00. Carmen does seem to know her way around the boat and helps untie the lines. I notice Carmen more than earlier in the day. She is strong, well built with smooth medium brown skin. Her hair is smoothed back to a single ponytail and she is wearing earrings designated for a calypso date out in the Caribbean. She does look a bit out of place. She looks worldly if I think about it. James drives us out and we go cruising out on the lake which is beginning to calm down. Not much wind and maybe we are in for a colorful sunset. James slows down, enters a cove, turns off the engine, and we all have a beer.

"To a beautiful cruise on the lake," says Angel.

"Cheers to a hell raising time," says the girlfriend named Carmen. I take a second look at her.

"To you both!" James gets to the point.

"And to a childless night," I add. Things feel a bit creepy at this moment and I don't know why. But I toast my drink and swallow some beer. James is looking at the couple as they are engaged in some serious lip tasting. I look away. One more day. Oh well. Relax. I close my eyes.

We are just floating in this little cove. I pull out dinner, the leftovers from yesterday, and we all fill our plates. Later on we head for the dock.

"Dinner was great. Thanks," says Angel.

"We will have a fire outside on the patio tonight if you want to join us," says James. That seems harmless.

"Sure, let us change and we'll join you."

CHAPTER THIRTY FIVE

When the couple reappears, Angel's girlfriend is wearing, I think, my boots and sweater. I took notice and declared, "I have the same boots and sweater, just like yours."

"Oh, these are yours!" She laughs.

"Hello, you didn't ask," I state with a silent '*bitch*' added for myself.

"You mind?"

"You could have asked."

"Megan, she probably didn't bring enough clothes. I suppose that's what happened," James says to make me feel easier about this.

"Oh, she brought enough clothes. You brought two suitcases for three nights, baby." Angel was trying to ease his girlfriend out of whatever he did not understand.

"Honey, I don't think we are welcome here." She says and comes right over to me and stands like it was a dare or something.

"You are welcome here, just don't take my clothes without asking!"

"You think you are high and mighty telling me how to act. I'll act, however, I want to act."

"You are a bitch," I say. I mean it. She was acting rude,

strutting around acting like she owns the place and taking my clothes without asking.

"Megan," says James.

"I can handle this," I say. I stand up and come face to face with this person I just met today and challenge her.

"Well, if it isn't the mom with no kids tonight ready for a duel."

"Who are you, besides rude?"

"Who am I?"

"Yeah, who are you?

"I'm the guest, asshole."

"Asshole?" I couldn't help but laugh, and make a fist with my hand, but then quickly realize I'm mad. Mad as hell. She has no right to come here as a guest and take my shit.

"You think you are perfect, the all perfect mother?"

"What on earth? You have gone crazy since this afternoon. You on drugs?" I shake my head at this unbelievable conversation. "What are we in high school?"

"Maybe. Maybe I am. You want some. I bet you do."

"No thanks. I think you should leave."

"Let's go baby. We are not welcome." She turns to Angel, pulls out a cigarette, lights it, then turns and blows smoke towards me.

Then she hands the cigarette to Angel, and tells me to come after her.

Unbelievably, I takes the bait. James is watching and not understanding any of this. Then again, this is not normal and he looks upon it like a show.

I choose to chase the girlfriend throughout the house running upstairs, through the hall, back down again, slamming doors, and making quite a ruckus I'm sure. She has me fired up.

The men are just looking in amazement until the

girlfriend comes back out and tells Angel to meet her at the car. She grabs the cigarette and he gets up to leave.

He stands in the way so I can't reach Carmen. He lets Carmen walk away like a cat who just stood down a dog.

Quickly, they depart to the car, get in, and are backing up the gravel drive in a hurried pace. Stones are flying, making thwarted sounds.

James and I come out the front and can't believe the bitch just stole my clothes. I raise my hands up in the air and then put them on my hips. "What the hell just happened? Why did you let her get away with that? You know she is wrong, such bad news!"

"Yeah. Wow." James just watches them and listens to the squeal of tires while they burn some rubber when they hit the pavement off of the stones.

"Quite an exit, I'd say."

"I'm going to put the fire out and clean up the kitchen. I don't understand." James looks perplexed.

"Me neither."

"Crazy bitch." He said it and I thought it.

In the morning I get up early, make coffee and blueberry pancakes for us. I want this day to be better. I don't understand last night and James doesn't help.

"I'm sorry about last night. Today will be better. She ticked me off with her rudeness and stealing."

"I get it, kind of. Strange though."

"Here have some breakfast, homemade blueberry pancakes. My favorite."

"My new favorite," he says. "Let me go get the paper. I see it on the driveway out front near the road."

We eat pancakes and drink coffee. I text my boys through the grandparents and James scours the newspaper.

"Well, here's a story."

"What?"

"It says the GBI thinks two murders are related, one from a Florida park where a teacher was murdered when she went jogging, and another gal from a park in North Georgia while taking her dogs for a walk."

"Really James? I don't need any more distractions right now. Missing women?"

"Oh, I'm sorry."

"What are you going to tell me next? That he came through Georgia and robbed the neighbors?" I point to the house that recently got robbed.

"Ah, yeah. How did you know?"

"What? No way. Tell me more." I shake my head in disbelief.

"It says the woman in North Georgia was murdered yesterday but they have linked it to another one in Florida. I'm sorry, I don't mean to scare you but you said you might want in on this type of business."

"I did say that, didn't I?"

"Yes. You did."

"I might change my mind. I might not have the stomach for it."

"Why?"

"After I saw that man in the grocery store yesterday I'm freaking out, and now you say he passed through here. More freaking out," I say almost out of breath.

"But wait, don't you see? You have a sixth sense, you can spot individuals that are up to no good."

"You think that's going to make me feel better right now?"

"I hope so. It's the truth. You've got it."

"Whatever it is ... I don't want it."

CHAPTER THIRTY SIX

James left the paper on the kitchen table with the headlines panned out for anyone to see. I was a scared-y cat. Why on earth was I contemplating a field of unknowns? Maybe I had '*it*.' Right now I wanted to forget about '*it*.'

We dress for dinner in elegant casual as we were going to The Lodge. We would have been going on a double date but we tried to forget about them. James said the place was a fixture near the lake. "It's an old wooden place with a deck and Elvis sings there."

"Elvis?"

"Well, not the real Elvis because he is dead but an improvisation, a guy who sings and dresses just like him." *This should be fun* I thought. And so I soon forgot about yesterday.

James was feeling a bit off himself and he most likely didn't want to be the one to scare me. Maybe he was testing me to see if I had it. I turned some music on, and turned to James. Once again, we swayed and moved and held each other close. Bliss. We could stay here all night but I needed to show off a little. You know I looked forward to walking in a swanky old place with my new man, my James.

As soon as we enter the dark, dimly lit atmosphere I could hear the singing and saw many couples dancing. There was a fireplace with a large framed picture of a man on a horse, such as in England, or South Carolina, I thought, going out on a hunt. At the horses hooves were several dogs, bird or hunting dogs, with one in particular that I took notice of. He had a white body with black spots and looked like a lovely pet. Below the mantel, the fireplace roared, and shown its light on the couples dancing on the wooden floor. Tables set about with booths and a large bar centered in the middle greeted you before the windows out back that looked out to a forest of pine trees.

We settle in and sit close. This is a perfect spot for a date as we nestle into our booth, order a martini, and look upon the menu. But first James said, "Let's dance before our drinks arrive."

And so we did.

We toast to each other after our dance and I thank him for picking such a cozy place near the lake.

"You're welcome!" He kisses me.

We share our dinner of scallops, shrimp, and filet mignon with a baked potato fully loaded pre-empted by a Cesar salad and little smoked cheddar bites. No we don't have room for dessert and the waiter asks us if we are ready for the check. I like this place, no hurry, no check before he asks. Excellent, I think. I'd come back here. I'd heard about it but had never been. How nice I got to spend it with James.

He gets a call before the check arrives and goes to answer it, only his phone goes dead. Just like that. We look at each other. What happened? Maybe his battery went dead. Then my phone rings from an unknown number. I don't answer it but see that I have a text from a local number that I don't recognize.

"Should I look at it?"

"Yes. Go ahead."

"It says ... We have someone at a special place you know very well."

James looks at me in question. "Let me see."

I hand him my phone.

He looks at it and reads it again. Then right before our eyes my phone dies.

"What on earth?"

"Let's go Megan. Let's get out of here."

"Are we being watched?"

"Yes."

"Oh no."

"Ready?"

I breathe in, begin to worry, shake my head from side to side and wonder. We leave in a hurry and head for the car.

Quickly, we escape, and speed off. I know where we are going.

"Back to the river we go. Why the river?"

"I would say that someone wants to kill more people. Wouldn't you?"

"But wouldn't it be marked off with yellow police tape by now and off limits?"

"Excellent question," James stated.

"Then why would we go there?"

"We won't."

"We won't?"

"What else did it say Megan?"

"A place I know very well."

"The message was to your phone about a place you know very well," said James.

"I don't know. What's going on?"

"Megan, what place do you know very well?"

"I don't know," I say.

"I'm supposing they want you to go to the river to stall you-no one will be there but you."

"The river, the marble house or shack, where the women were killed."

"I think they want you away from the lake house, away from the crime." James states. He is sure I can tell.

"Why is this happening?"

"We are in the middle of a sting, Megan. I'm sorry but we'll just have to do our best. You're protected. Stay with me. We'll be fine."

"We are protected, then how come you don't know very much?" I have to ask this insane question because nothing is making sense.

"Once again, very good question! Because people at the top are betting on someone doing something wrong and they'll catch them red handed."

"Maybe someone is bugging your car?"

"Boy are you learning fast, except I had it debugged earlier today. Clean as a whistle."

"I didn't tell you this but I have been practicing using a gun for two weeks now."

"I know."

James swerves around a corner going too fast. The tires squeal and my head hits the window.

"Hey."

"Sorry."

The night is dark and I seem to have been energized with this reckless car driving by James. We don't know who has who but somebody wants me away for a while, maybe James too. I suspect James has an idea but is trusting his higher ups to protect him. Just in case, I'll arm myself with one of his guns. I saw that he packed them; I felt the metal from the outside of his backpack when I put it away.

He speeds right into the gravel drive and we exit the car quickly, running into the house. Immediately it doesn't feel right as we go through the door.

We both look up to the loft and see Angel sitting in a chair all tied up. Two other bodies are close by watching him. You can see the silhouettes from the moon glow through the glass.

The couple has returned, only they aren't so lovey-dovey at the moment. The bitch woman seems to be in charge asking the questions, demanding the other guy to answer her.

"How you going to do this? Tell me!" Carmen shouts.

Apparently, they didn't hear us come in.

"I told you. I'll make it look like a suicide, like he became distraught because you ditched him."

James and I hide from sight and listen. James recognizes the guy's voice. It was Joe, the brother of Mickey, the cop that shot his girlfriend at the river in the old shack. James quiets me and points to the back bedroom where he keeps his guns. We tread lightly without notice.

"Then what?" I hear Carmen ask Joe.

"What do you mean what?" Joe replies.

"What about the couple who rented the place? I met them earlier today."

"We got plenty of time as I sent her a message to go to the river."

"How did you accomplish that? That's good. That will give us maybe a couple hours or so."

"My boss. He takes care of the spy shit, I just take care of business." Joe confesses.

"Why you let me in on this?" Carmen asks a great question.

"Because my brother is out of the business and I need

some help out here. Got to make the dough, you know."

"Yeah, I know." She acts like this is a norm.

"There's plenty of it though."

"How do you know?" *Again a great question by Carmen* I think.

"My boss is in on the insurance deals. They are raking in the green and they pay him off if they don't have to pay out a big sum."

"Why this young guy?"

"I asked the same question."

"And?"

"Because his life is worth a lot; he's got a rich momma. I've been searching for him for a long time." Joe concedes again.

"Why not just kidnap and ask for ransom?"

"Because suicide equals no pay out. Period. Insurance companies like that. Certain rich people have to pay large amounts up front; he's one of those. Plus this kid owes me for what he took a few years back."

"You mean the scammers, or the mob?" Carmen is a smart woman, though a bitch, I think.

"Yeah, the insiders."

"Your boss, he's an insider?" Carmen doesn't let up. She's a badass I'm thinking. Take notes Megan.

"All the way up the ladder, never met him. He just gives us the work."

CHAPTER THIRTY SEVEN

I had the gun in my hand and this made me a little shaky. Maybe I wasn't fully ready for these shenanigans. Only this was real right upstairs in the loft. *Do your best* I told myself. I look at James and that's when I trip over a misplaced toy. Down I went ... and the gun fell out of my hand as I had to soften my fall. The gun went off too.

"Watch him. I'll go see what's downstairs."

"You might need back up," Joe said.

"I can handle it," said Carmen as she readied her gun and flew down the stairs. She grabbed me immediately and pulled me to my feet by my hair. This was not a good position to be in and by her of all people.

"Look at what I found," she said quite aloud for all to hear. I had no idea where James was at this point. But I was headed up the stairs and in control by another woman for the second time in as many months.

At the top of the stairs I could plainly see, even in the dark, the boyfriend named Angel. He looked distraught to say the least and I wanted desperately to help him. Here the bitch had me, and it seems has turned him over to the bad cop. What the hell was going on? Was this part of the plan? Don't worry-remember James said he had it all covered. Yeah right. That's how much trust I had in him at this moment. I told myself I'd go to real training if I ever got out of this mess.

She presented me to Joe who looked me over. "Yeah, I been following you for a while you little mother fucker. Quite pretty outside of the camera."

I look at him and want to spit in his face or kick him in the balls, maybe both. If I had the gun right now I might want to shoot him. "Is that right mother fucker?" I say with the best mother fucking New York accent I can put out, like I'm some kind of mob queen.

"Oh look, what language comes out when you're scared?" He retorts with macho filled sarcasm.

"Scared, don't think so. Mad as hell. They are coming for you, you ass."

"Who's coming for me? James? Maria? You don't have anyone coming for you. I made sure of it."

I shut up while I thought about what he just said. Carmen winked at me. They don't think he is here. They think he is somewhere else. But where? Why did she wink at me?

"Guess he went to the river and you came home to safety, huh?" Carmen said.

"Yes, but he'll be here when he realizes no one is there!" I exclaim.

"But dear, we'll be all done." Joe says.

I watch him as she holds the gun to my heart. She made me sit on the pool table while I had to listen to him go on and on about his business.

He walks back and forth strumming his own tune about what he was going to do with the money he was about to make. He even explains he'd overheard his boss talking about the operation and other clients he had. He mentioned how big the spying game really was getting. Murderers got off all the time he said. I felt like I was being privy to the master mobster. I didn't have to wonder what he was going to do with me as he got directly on that.

"Miss Megan, you were in the wrong place at the wrong time. That's the matter with you."

"I was in the right place at the right time, mother fucker," I said in the most bad ass way I could.

He took notice. "Well, look at that courage right before the dawn of the end."

"What?"

"You will be gone. But before you go away, forever, I want you to know something."

"What's that you filthy scum?"

"My, my, so wordy aren't we?" The fat bellied cop was way over his head, bragged too much, and definitely was going down tonight. For that I was sure.

I look around the room to find something I could use to escape since I didn't have a gun. Where this sudden bravery came from I did not know.

"You were supposed to be dead already. My boss put a hit out on you, but they missed, backed out. Seems our hired hit man couldn't kill a mom with three kids. Guess he took a liking to you. Lucky you but now your luck has run out." He laughs. His belly shook and I wished I had a gun I'd kill him right now, the piece of shit.

Suddenly, he had drawn me in. I knew what I saw and believed in myself. I was right all along. This was no baby cakes plan. This was bigger than TV, it was real. People really did this shit, unbelievable. But why? Silly me, if we knew that then we wouldn't be here. Get on with it. Get yourself out of here. Oh boyfriend, where are you?

"Carmen, watch them for a minute."

She nodded. He went to use the bathroom. Some idiot

has to use the bathroom while he's doing a double murder. I look at her and when she heard the door close she put her finger to her lip and winked. Angel saw it, too. What now I shrugged?

She put five fingers in the air and then smacked me across the face. "Stay where you are I said!"

"Bitch!"

"That's right, you piece of shit."

Out of the corner of my eye I see movement downstairs outside on the bricked patio. Back up has arrived. *About time* I tell myself. I need to get out of this mess. I want out. Help. Straighten up Meg, no tears.

"All right Carmen, it's almost show time."

"This little mother tried to escape but no not tonight." *Carmen was playing the game too well*, I thought.

"Good girl, you and I are going to make a good team. A few years of this and we both can retire, live the good life, somewhere." Big cop Joe retorted and then coughed a bit.

"You know boss if I'm going to kill her, and suicide him, I'd like to give praise to the higher up, especially with all the money I'll be collecting."

"And it will be plenty, rest assured. I've made over two hundred grand already these past couple years. Just want to make another hundred and I'm gone."

"Yeah, I like the sound of that. I always wanted to work my way higher up."

"I can put a good word in for you. Mr. Freesia runs the show from the CIA. They had a little trouble a few weeks ago but it's still in business, bigger than ever they tell me."

"Appreciate that my fellow cop," says, Carmen. And then without further comments she goes into a commander role and begins issuing orders. It all happens so fast I can't see straight. I see a smoke bomb down below and many guys outside while she tackles Joe. She takes down Joe while someone is here undoing Angel from the chair. The next thing I know someone has come to my side and is telling me how brave I am. Then, like the newbie sleuth I am, I faint. I know it.

CHAPTER THIRTY EIGHT

The Special Forces arrive and I miss all the action! The ending. I woke up an hour or so later in bed. Someone tells me everything. I check my phone which happens to be lying next to me on the nightstand. I was dizzy and felt weak. I look up and there are two officers, both undercover in my room. Where is James?

"Where's James?"

"He's okay. He's outside talking to the boss." One of the female undercover cops tells me.

"Thanks."

"Sure. Can I get you anything?"

"You like your job?" I ask.

"Absolutely. I worked my way up through several positions. Now I'm almost there."

"Sounds like a plan to work your way up the chain, so you aren't afr ..."

Undercover officer interlude ...

"She fell asleep again. Too much trauma, "says the undercover police officer.

"Watch her, I'm going to go check on James, in case she wakes again and wants to know."

Megan wakes …

I awaken to hear James talking on the phone, sitting on the edge of the bed next to me. He has the phone on speaker.

"James, excellent work." Says the apparent woman and super spy on the other end.

"I'm not sure I did much Scarlet. I think you should be thanking that girlfriend cop, she did all the work. She's quite an actress, too."

"You kept the team altogether, that's what an expert does."

"Thank you. Glad to be of service. Now about my boss. Is he in on it?"

"No, I mean he's undercover like you. But *his* boss knew everything going on for a couple years. We got loads of info, more than we planned on."

"Good. Take care of the bad guys and let me know what you need next." James is sincere.

"Tell me what the three pictures were of behind my sofa on the wall." She was persistent I could tell.

"Sure. For some reason you have a Boy with a Boot, a young male painter, and Christopher Columbus, I presume."

"See, you are good. Train that Megan and we'll have more jobs for you James, maybe even in the art world." She laughs. He doesn't know if she is joking or not.

"She won't be ready for a while and she's looking for part time anyway as she has three kids."

"Yes, I know. Sounds good. When you visit Maria, don't say anything about me. I'd like to keep my distance on that."

"I imagine they will be changing some outcomes or the way they do business."

"All of this in the name of terrorism and freedoms. Back and forth we go. It's definitely a juggling act, spying and not being too invasive. Then again we have to stay ten steps ahead of them."

"How many Joe's are out there doing the wrong thing?" Scarlet listens to James intently and wants to know this more than anything.

She replies. "We are finding out. That is one of my principal causes and I'm in until the end. It gives me great joy to applaud the servicemen and women that honestly and bravely do their job to protect the American people. Then when I get the bad apple, I tell my dead husband I did that for him."

"I'm glad Nate introduced me to you. I look forward to meeting you again someday."

"Likewise. Night."

"Night."

James presses his phone off. I really need to speak to him as I am a bit overwhelmed.

"What else do you suppose they were doing to Americans through dragnet spying? I'm sure other information like health, and insurance purchases were unloaded in their espionage undertaking, even bank deposits given as gifts were investigated."

"I suppose we will never know all of it. And much of it is still ongoing."

"Oh, my imagination will come up with quite a bit I'm sure. Lately, I can't stop thinking about weird things or mysterious happenings." I feel like talking.

"You should rest and we can talk in the morning." James adds.

"I can't stay here anymore you know. Too much occurred. Too many what ifs?"

"I get it." James implies his sincerity.

"What should we do? We still have two weeks left."

"How about we stay for the daytime tomorrow then pack. I have a great idea."

"Do tell. That way I can think of a bright spot, a white light instead of all these murders."

"We could go to Destin."

CHAPTER THIRTY NINE

"How will we get down there? Drive or fly?" I ask "How do you want to go?" James replies.

"I don't care." I seem to be in a don't care state of mind. I don't have to wonder why.

"Since we have extra time-let's drive. That way you'll see the countryside on the way down and cross the bridge before we arrive."

"Will we go deep sea fishing?"

"You bet, for sure."

"We should go see Maria tomorrow at the hospital."

"I talked with her and she's better. Her mother and daughter are there with her."

"That's good."

"Tell me why does a person who works in law enforcement go badly?"

"Maybe they have a tendency to do things wrong to begin with."

"What did he gain by participating?"

"Money, that's it. Jail time, too."

"Let me get this straight, so I understand. Somewhere way up the chain a guy gets money from insurance, a scam, so that the company doesn't have to pay out upon someone's death. It has to be already collected for a while and a large amount put upfront by the rich."

"Somebody rich like Angel's mother who could afford to have a large policy on her son. If he commits suicide, then there's no payout to her or anyone else."

"Yes, that's it. But I have a feeling this was part of the sting-to catch the bad guys. We just laid the foundation for the setup, since they knew Joe was following you."

"I was being followed?"

"Tapped and followed, that's why I couldn't tell you everything. You understand we needed you to act natural and do your normal things."

"First they went after Maria to make her go crazy, sort of, what they didn't bet on was the sick girlfriend of the new cop-Joe's brother which was Maria's ex. He was not in on anything like his brother."

"The girl all dressed out named Rebekka who dueled me."

"They didn't know she would go crazy and follow Maria or kill the other two gals they were tapping. I guess they didn't keep their business too secretive, except Joe's brother didn't know any of it. He was new and trying to do the right thing. He saved your life."

"I know. But what a scumbag treating Maria like shit before he became a cop. He might not keep the job I'm told."

"He is under review and I have a feeling that since he lied he won't be trusted or back on active duty, but rather he might come back or work in the office. He was actually a good cop. He must have had a coming to Jesus moment or revelation. Some people do change when given a chance, you just don't know who will."

"I am grateful for him saving my life; he didn't hesitate and did the right thing."

"I have to tell you one more thing."

"Yes?"

"Your sixth sense thing you have, intuition or whatever, seems to be accurate. I believe you."

"Why?"

"Because the top boss told me it's almost certain that you were targeted as a hit. I don't know why he didn't go through with it. Usually those types are severe, they don't back off as they are getting paid. They don't care."

"Do go on."

"The guy you saw in the grocery store was the hit man," James said the words.

"Oh no, " I shiver and my nerves take the circuit full throttle. I had to stand up. "Seriously?"

"I'm sorry."

I pace the floor.

"Why?"

"Just to be rid of you. I told you they are ruthless " I could tell James did not even want to tell me this. "With you out of the way-then Maria was an easier target."

"But he's gone now. They got him. Right?"

"Absolutely, without a doubt. They got him."

"Good."

"And what about the sting on our first date? Did you figure that one out yet?"

"The guys that are training you in the gym with swords are working on that hit. They surveilled the place that night I took you back there to see who might be in on that."

"Really?"

"Yes. It was a payoff for a service, then kill the guy anyway, go back, and get your money back. Scammers scamming the whole scam. Then it looks like bad guys do all the bad work, yet somebody hired them to do it. Bad business."

"There's a whole other world out there-I want to help you James from the inside."

"I want you to be safe from harm," he says.

"I can learn to be more like Carmen. What a badass!"

"She's almost fearless." James smiles.

"I just need a touch of that, or maybe I can turn that on when I want to."

"And turn it off when you don't need it."

"I have to forget some of these things and not let it bother me. I have to turn it off. Soon."

James comes to me and hugs me good.

"You can go on. You can forget all about it."

"Like a switch I must turn it off."

CHAPTER FORTY

We pack up and James heads down to the dock. It was a shame that this beautiful lake house would go to waste. I just couldn't shrug, Carmen, and fellow cop, Joe, with guns to my heart, Angel all tied up, followed by smoke bombs below, tackling, and the passing out on my part. Maybe I wasn't cut out for this line of work, or maybe I would have to be a cop first. I didn't know but James told me to forget about it right now. It would come to us what is the right thing to do.

I look out the window over at the neighbor's house when I see two guys park a car, get out, and retrieve something out of the trunk. *Forget about them and go pack a lunch for one last boat ride* I tell myself. I head to the kitchen and make some peanut butter and jelly sandwiches. I make a couple extra as there is too much food left over. I feel kind of bad we are leaving but in retrospect James probably knew once the sting was over we would be leaving.

I startle and feel my nerves jump when I hear a chain saw roar up, over, and over. Then a few moments later my doorbell rings. Oh no, who could that be? I am so rattled. Watch out whomever you are I just might explode!

I have to answer it. Whomever it is knows I'm in here. I make my way to the front door and hear the chain saw go gangbusters again. Shut up already. It must be my nerves. Goosebumps follow my chilly mind. I take a deep breath, exhale, and open the door.

I've died and been delivered into the movie 'Deliverance.'

"Hey mam, you need some trees cut?" He slashes the wind with his hand showing his skill then his eyes light up further. I stare and stare some more.

I look at the two of them and realize I am in the south. They are for real. One is tall with thin long hair and very skinny but taut to the bones. I barely catch his name. His eyes rove everywhere. There is a cigarette dangling from his lips. I look over at his shorter buddy and he has one eye. I want to ask what happened but decide I don't want to know. Maybe it was the cigarette from his boss. I shudder. I stare and then try not to stare. They are probably nice people, just hungry maybe. I think I'll offer them my extra sandwiches. And whatever you do don't tell them you are in the house alone right now. Got it Megan! I want to look at the floor right now thinking that I must be standing in a pool of blood, my own. For surely they have hacked or cut me in half. Don't faint.

"Thanks guys, but no, I don't need any trees cut down. Leave me a card and I'll call when I do."

The tall guy wrote his name on a card with a pencil and handed it to me. It held his phone number too.

"Thanks. Wait one minute, I'll be right back." I closed the door because, enough drama already, and ran to the kitchen to grab the sandwiches. Shame on me for thinking such backwoods thoughts about people. Megan, they are what they are! I ran back to the door.

When I open the door my movie stood before me as I was transplanted to another time, another vision of some movie maker's experience. Except this was real. I shake my head. "Guys, I made some extra sandwiches a bit ago, please have these."

"Thanks." The guy with one eye said, something like that anyway, and grabbed the sandwiches, turned away, and moved off of the porch.

"Call me mam, you've got some trees back ways will soon fall, hit the house when the storm comes."

"Storms, you're right. I'll call you soon."

"Later." He took a drag from his cigarette, smiled with his glassy eyes at me, and walked away.

Megan, close the door. Now. I did. But I went to watch them walk back to the neighbors drive, retrieve some belts, and gloves, maybe more cigarettes and walk to the back of the house. Why was I spooked?

I settle back in the kitchen and finish making our lunch for the last picnic at this beautiful lake house, then I heard the chain saws explode their force. This time I wasn't scared like half an hour ago. They were just some backwoods tree cutters here to make the places safe from the storms. Or were they? How my mind seemed to expand upon ordinary things. Most likely, logically, because you have seen some things that Poe writes about, dreams and such. I did talk with one person for an hour after the attack and murders at the marble quarry. It could likely be my mind and thoughts might think more evil is coming my way, it may take a few months she said to quiet down. That is normal, after all, you experienced real trauma. The blood I saw was real and I dueled some bitch that died falling on me from a bullet hole to the head. Yeah, I'd say Poe might have something to say to me for a while. Dream or no dream, go check on them one more time. And so I did.

The bathroom had a laundry room attached so I could look out three different windows towards the neighbors. I did. The guys were out back busy working on trees. The other view was the lake and I could see James down at the dock cleaning up the boat and putting things away.

Finally, I check on the neighbor's drive and I could see the woodsmen's auto. I focus trying to see what was lying near the back window. It was a hat. It was a police officer's hat. What?

My mind rattles my nervous being again. Good cop or bad cop? Did they kill a cop? Or were they off duty police officers? Come on Megan, they don't look like officers. Or do they? They must be making a movie around here. Get a grip. That's when I see James's phone and I pick it up. I open it as he gave me his code during this trip. How nice. I select addresses and hit Nate's number.

"Hello, James, what's up?"

"Nate, its Megan."

"Megan dear, what can I do for you?"

"We are still at the lake house."

"I know."

"Well, there's a car next door with some tree cutter guys doing work in the woods."

"Yes."

"I can see a police cap in the back window."

"Ok."

"Why is that?"

"I don't know. You tell me."

"No Nate, you tell me."

"Hey Megan, I will look into it."

"Do it soon, okay?"

"Very soon."

"Thanks. Bye."

"Bye Megan."

I load up a cooler with sandwiches, dip and chips, beer,

water, and a couple cookies left from the boy's time here. There's even some watermelon, I add ice to the plastic baggie to keep it cold. I put on my suit, grab a towel, and then head down towards the plank way to board the boat on the dock.

Of course, I nonchalantly look over at the boys cutting trees. Nate will figure it out for me, so I don't bother about being worried. I relax, no prickly goosebumps skin. We are going to have a superb day on the lake, and later, like tomorrow morning, head to Destin. Relax Megan, things are looking up.

"Hey Megan, I was wondering what was taking you a while? I left my phone and couldn't call you."

"I packed us a nice picnic. I want to relax and enjoy the day, maybe get a little tan or slight sunburn."

"Okay, she's ready to rock and roll. Let's go."

I open a beer for both of us. Eleven o'clock in the am, no problem. We are on vacation. Let's party I think to myself. What's that? It had been years as in seven or eight years. I deserve a nice guy, a boat ride, and a generous amount of me time.

"Here you go captain," I say to James.

"Thanks mate," he replies.

CHAPTER FORTY ONE

James finds us a private little cove. He anchors, and I open up our snacks. We have a beer, eat some snacks, and go for a swim. Then we dry off, get some sun, and listen to his blue tooth music selections from the single speaker. It's a jam tape he made quite a while ago. He said he listened to certain music when he was in active seal training.

"Let me apply some sunscreen for your back," says my honey.

"Sure, I need to put it all over."

We lay on the deck of the boat listening to music drinking some beer and time stops. Just like that. We swim and then repeat the whole thing over again plus we kiss a good while.

All was sweet until ... the sound returned like a scratch on an old record just bound to make you get up and do something.

I sat up and heard the noise from this morning. It was coming towards us.

James asks, "What is it? You recognize it?"

"I think it's the tree cutters. Listen."

Then right around the bend in the lake and towards our little cove the two men came motoring in our space on the lake. I stare in disbelief. James held my hand as he could see

I was becoming upset.

Their little boat slows down and heads right for us. Slowly it cruises right past us and the two back woodsmen look upon us with their outrageous personas. The tall skinny guy with a cigarette in his mouth shook his head up and down as he acknowledges us while captaining his little motor boat. The one eyed blind man revs up his chain saw on battery power making the loud obnoxious powerful noise.

James gives a wave, a salute of sorts, and I just watch in disbelief. Really? *Where are you going besides disrupting my space* I question.

The boat lands on shore and they pull it up, no anchor but tie it to a tree. They depart and walk into the woods with their equipment, extension cords and all, connected to their battery.

"Must be a property up there they are working on."

"Like you only get to it by boat?" I ask loud and rude.

"I suppose so."

We head back to the dock and try not to let the guys ruin our day. James laughs at me just a little. He told me to not be afraid of these guys. They are harmless. I repeat his words but not really sure I believe them.

We pack up, and leave, and are off to visit Maria.

As we pull away I can't help but look back at the neighbors, the car in the drive with the police cap, and think that this whole business is not over. My instincts kick in and tell me there's more. I wonder if Nate knows more. I think he would advise James if he knew. I tell myself to keep up my guard, be on the lookout, let James train you, and join him if you can. I need police training though. That's the first thing I should do. I'll sign up after this vacation, get a loan, and go to school when the twins enter 2nd grade, and my eight year old enters 3rd grade. My resolve to gain employment is there, the timing is accurate with the boys in school. We could all study at night together. I feel so good about this I smile.

"Why so happy Megan?"

"I figured out what I am going to do."

"Can you tell me?"

"Sure. You can help me."

"Okay. What are you going to do?"

"I'm going to go back to school. I'll need your advisement."

"School? What kind?"

"I'll need some training, you know law enforcement, under cover PI stuff, or maybe FBI investigations."

"Basically, you don't know what kind of operative you want to be."

"Nailed it." I point my finger at him.

"Sure, I'll help. We can talk about it when we go fishing in the Gulf," James says earnestly.

I smile. This was a new direction for me and I like it. My boys and I would be busy and I'd save the weekends for James. I have to admit I sound like I'm conquering Mt. Everest, or solving the Boston Strangler case, but in essence I just feel stronger physically and mentally by making a commitment.

CHAPTER FORTY TWO

We visit Maria after leaving the lake house. We don't need to stop by my place or his as we were going to be gone for three weeks anyhow. We stop at the book store and buy her a gift, a book, and some stationery items for her daughter, Hope, in addition to a card.

Finally, we make it to the mini hospital, Howard Hotel, and knock on the back door. They recognize us and let us in. We sign in and make our way up the stairs to her room. It's open and we walk in after a light knock. Maria gets up from the table, sees that it is us, smiles, and comes to give us a big hug!

"Maria, you look well," I say.

"I'm so happy to see you guys. I've missed you."

"You do look very well. No more nightmares?" James asks.

"Now and then I wake up but I am fine, very comfortable here. But it is time to go home."

"When do you get released?" I ask.

"Two days."

"Perfect, you will have the place to yourself. We are heading in the opposite direction and going to the beach."

"I did hear you went to a lake house with the boys," Maria says.

"We had a fabulous time and decided to go see where James wants to move to."

"You want to move to the beach?"

"Maybe in a year or two," he replies.

"I should move there, too." She says with the biggest smile on her face. Then she turns to her mother and Hope over at the table. "How about we move to the beach next year?"

"Momma, that sounds super. I love the ocean. We could go swimming every day and look for turtles, and fish, and dolphins!"

"She likes the idea. Me too."

"Can you go for a walk outside Maria?"

"Yes, let's go. We can go down to the garden out back."

We head outside after letting them know where we'll be.

Its lovely outback and you can walk and look at all the flowers and different plants. It is like a mini outdoor museum.

I didn't bring her out here to talk about anything untoward or unusual. I just wanted to see if she was comfortable leaving her immediate surroundings and she was.

"Megan, I am going to be fine. I have never felt better."

"I believe you. I do."

"The doctor told me that I would remember everything eventually, and to talk about it but don't focus on it. I am alive for a reason and to run with that. That and my family, daughter and mother, we will all be fine."

We hold hands and hug each other. "You can stay with me as long as you like. I know we were all thinking you needed to move out and be on your own, but I love the company so I'm extending the stay."

"Gracias Megan, and we will. We would love to stay

with you until I find a job after my schooling. I appreciate your kindness."

"You're welcome."

"I do love seeing you two together! There's hope for me, maybe."

James and I smile and feel great hearing her say those words after the turmoil she suffered from her ex-husband, and, of course, the psycho bitch from the marble quarry near the river.

We walk around going down a couple paths. We smile again at one another and I apologize. "I'm so sorry Maria that I didn't take what you were saying more seriously. I had no idea people could infiltrate your life and make it hell."

"Neither did I."

"We are all going to live a more guarded life but still enjoy it." James spoke up.

"He'll teach us how to do that."

I give her a big hug and kiss her cheek. She does the same in return. James hugs us both.

We say goodbye and tell her we'll see her in about two weeks.

"Take care honey." I say.

"You two do the same."

It takes us six hours to get to the beach. It is breathtaking. We unload and head for our condo on the third floor overlooking the gulf.

The rental lady from the lake house gave us a full refund to use whenever we wanted and/or when it was available. Kindness. She understood our plight and was very grateful it all worked out.

We head to dinner down at the harbor and sign up for a fishing trip the day after tomorrow. After dinner we get a few groceries and unpack all our goods. We are tired. The only thing on our minds is sleep.

CHAPTER FORTY THREE

First thing in the morning after waking, James's phone rings, as we are out in the kitchen getting coffee and breakfast. He says, "Hello, how are you?"

James and I sit down on the sofa where the view looks out over the sea, he puts the phone on speaker. "I've got you on speaker, you can fill both of us in on all the events, and catch us up to date."

"Oh. Hello, Megan and James. Are we a team now?"

"We are an unofficial team. She wants to join the blue boys and do great things."

"And you are going to train her, James?"

"You and me are going to train her," says James.

"Lucky me," I say.

"Oh sweetie, we are the lucky ones." Nate unleashes his grace, a bit worldly for working in a small shop. Of course, I knew nothing about him.

There was a slight pause as we drank some coffee and ate our breakfast. The view kept getting in our way. "If you could see our view Nate, you'd want to join us right now."

"Oh, but lovelies, I can see your view. Don't ask."

James shakes his head.

"Give us the updates."

"Well, I have another assignment as soon as you are

done with your vacation. We will not interrupt this one. Scarlet feels bad that the timing was off and y'all had to run to the beach."

"Go on."

"We got more information and arrests than we had planned on. The scope of the insurance fraud was pretty big, and a nasty bunch of individuals running the madness."

"Glad we could help, but your undercover cop did most of it."

"She's a good one. Almost too good with her theatrics, I know."

"Totally believable let me add," I say.

"She'll probably have to move to another state, so she can keep her cover for a longer time."

"Scarlet has her boy back in school and she is happy."

"Tell me about the next assignment." James instructs.

"Not going to give you too much-that way you won't over think the situation. It needs to be fresh when you start. However, the old lady wants to see you when she finishes up her treatment and gets her health back on track. She asked me if you believed her."

"Yes, I did."

"I told her no problem. Of course, you believed her and want to help her. She says she will be in treatment for six months, then she can see you three months after that as it takes that long to recover from the special poison they give her."

"Think her information will lead to anything?"

"That's what I'm working on right now. I've got leads but I want indictments, you know bad shit. The world is too crazy right now and we need the bad criminals before it gets out of hand."

"Sounds great, I would love to see her again. But

remember she wasn't sure she would make it past this treatment," I add.

"This assignment will probably be mostly paperwork, checking security systems and personnel. This will be a good one for Megan to learn on. Less physical and bloody, more covert operations, and infringement of rights, civil liberties, etc."

"Now, James, let me talk with you for a moment about the ones we caught."

"Sure."

"Bye Nate, thanks."

James mostly listens and takes in what Nate is saying. He looks over at me one time and I could see a pause for concern. Hopefully that was nothing. Then he says goodbye and hangs up.

"Oh, I forgot I wanted to ask him about the tree cutters that I saw before we left."

"Come here sweetie. We'll talk shop tomorrow on the boat."

"Okay. Must have been nothing."

James never felt more luscious since we first made love and connected. I had to admit it had been quite a wonderful ride since our first date. Everyone had gotten along at the lake, James and the boys, before they left. They had called earlier tonight after dinner missing me. That felt good. They were still so cute. They even wanted to talk with James. Then after dinner we went for a swim in the pool. We had to get up early in the morning with a deep sea charter out of The Harbor.

The view was perfect from the kitchen and family room area in our condo. We were only on the third floor-so we could walk outside to the pool and back again in moments. Our room was decorated in light ocean blues and medium wooden colored tones, accented with ropes, or lines as James called them. The sea view pictures gave sense of the nautical boutique stores which lined the harbor walkway.

We dance a little with hugs before settling into the bed.

"I love you," I say.

"I love you, too."

Morning came and we prepared for a day at sea. I am super excited to go out on the ocean with this guy I have fallen in love with. There's that love sequence about doing new things with a special person and he did not disappoint. What would happen today?

The wind was blowing mightily and even I knew that might not be perfect weather for fishing. But we went anyway, no refunds I guess unless a verified storm. I drank my coffee and ate a donut. Very simple, not much at 5:30 am. James did as well. We brought our light packed lunch with sandwiches and drinks.

It is magnifying beautiful to be out on the water when the sun is rising after the boat has left shore. The buildings rise higher, the clouds more discernable, and the smiles unforgettable. We sit and watch our crew work hard just for us. It felt cozy inside the fishing boat with the deep water getting more prominent as the shore dissipated from view. Our trust is placed in the captain, and crew, of course.

There was eight of us aboard, all couples of sorts. I had boated but not like James. But I did know enough that on a day like today anyone could get sick. It didn't mean you weren't the ship type or didn't possess sea legs. I honestly didn't think I would but something about watching the first to go outside lowers your threshold. Mine was lowered and no matter what I did the feeling lay there like "hey little missy, you are not getting out of this one." I try to will it away as I don't want to be the prissy little woman on board today.

"Pardon me, I'm going out back." I walk on sea legs to get to the door. It was rough out here. I had waited and waited, thinking the sea would calm after we got out here but it didn't. I could not imagine what the captain way up in the bird's nest was experiencing going side to side. I looked back at James. He sat there calmly not looking at me. Good thing. We don't need both of to get ill. One has to be superior-let it be him.

Once I opened the door it was all I could do to stay upright and make my way back to the corner of the boat. Waves were splashing inside making the deck more slippery than usual. But I made my way all the way to the back and held on tight. I certainly didn't want the captain turning around to retrieve me. Or a worst case scenario that I enter the deep waters of the Gulf with five footers and a shark find me instead. Hold on tight for dear life. My spirit is more important than any vomit. I let it rip, couldn't even see it but two spills and it was all out. Not much, but wow, I smiled. Happiness. I'm better. Okay my pride is returning. It happens to the best of them. I guess I'm a lady after all. Here I thought I was a god damn tomboy my whole life. I'm a girl, well, just at this moment. Lord you can return my bad ass shit right now. I looked out over the silver bluish ocean in all its enormity, and I fell in love with the water. Right there. It was saying to me I'm your friend, I'll watch out for you. Always.

I take a deep breath and walk inside. We still have an hour or more to get out to the fishing spots. One of the guys starts talking with us-betting who might catch a mackerel or a dolphin. Everyone chips in a buck towards the winner. The conversation took our minds off the swells which came at us even harder out here. The boat seemed to want to go on its side. James said we would be fine. He said this was a very rough day for sure. It would not bother the fishing only our stance outside on deck with our poles. I was in for some exercise today. This was going to be work. The deck hands showed us the ropes and I had no problem baiting with squid, the slimy squid. Drop, hit bottom, come up a cast or two and wait. Wait for fish on, then reel it in, guide it over to the deck hand without hitting him in the head, and they'd take your fish off. Sounds good. And stay upright with pole in hand and the other to support yourself with the large sways.

It works. We caught so many fish I lost count. Then we reel up the lines and scurry off to the next area. The captain was using a fish finder and he knew what he was doing. During one of the tours to another spot-the casting pole gave way to a big fish. He runs out there and everyone watches as he reels in a King Mackerel. Next time it was another's turn, and so forth, and so forth. We caught three King Mackerel and a Mahi Mahi. All of us stood out there watching the big catches from the trolling rods. The Mahi Mahi was a beauty. He told us to take the picture of the beautiful yellow and blue fish, immediately, as it would soon wither its colors and fade to greys. I didn't know this. We watch it as it does this. After a while it resembles the King Mackerel, all grey and white, with a speared bloody gash from the deck hands push to secure it aboard. My, my. This is quite a day!

I have to say this was by far one of the best days of my life. It's worth every penny to go deep sea fishing-there is just nothing like it in all the world. It was expensive and not everyone is willing to put forth that kind of dough. The whole idea way out there where you can't see land, and you are dependent upon the captain for your safety, it's a glorious wonderful time. Someday, I decide, I would have to take my boys.

After a long while the captain cruises at a slower trolling pace. We then set about to eat our lunch and drink whatever we brought with us. This time the swells were not as large as we head towards the land, instead they were behind us giving us a nudge like on a slow ride at an amusement park.

I put the meat and cheese on a slice of bread and buttered the other slice with mayo right out of the jar. James had cut a few tomatoes and I place one on each sandwich. We ate and swallow down the meal with a beer. We were boating, fishing, and loving the great outdoors! I instantly feel at home on this big fishing boat-I can see why he wants to move down here and be next to the ocean.

On the way back James falls asleep and lays his head on my lap. I put my head against the window and rest as well. Once at the dock the deck hands slice and filet our fish we caught. We take ours with us to cook later. We decide to go back and get cleaned up for a nice meal at a place near the bridge on Harbor Walk.

We arrive late for lunch and too early for dinner. But that bothers neither one of us.

"What would you like to drink Megan?"

"Surprise me."

James orders for both of us.

I contemplate our catch from the deep sea fishing excursion, and how the Mahi Mahi or dolphin fish loses its glorious color, turning pale grey and white. The blood stays red but the skin color dissipates like it's seen a ghost. Quite extraordinaire!

We look out from the second floor dining room to the harbor in every direction.

"It's incredible. Everywhere I look something is happening."

"It's like that. Busy. Busy. Busy."

I look over by the bridge and boats are coming and going in so many directions. Lights are strewn along the water's edge illuminating the forth coming night. Our drinks arrive. James has ordered me a vodka tonic with lime. Refreshing. He has a bourbon. We toast. Our glasses clink. While I'm thinking of a toast he surprises me.

"To three King Mackerel and a Mahi Mahi!"

"I know you have a special meaning behind that. Please tell me," I insist.

"When you begin training my dear, I'll tell you everything you need to know."

The End